SHE STALKS THE LONELY back alleys and harbor docks of Boston, killing vampires one by one in revenge for her mother's murder.

Armed with a wooden stake, martial arts, and the will to resist a vampire's mind control, she is safe as long as her true identity remains a secret.

But when she rescues a girl from certain death, Rashel is suddenly swept into the Night World slave trade, gateway to the vampires' secret enclave. Here the gatekeeper is the dark, dangerous, and irresistible Quinn. He holds the keys to the realm Rashel is desperate to enter. But when she looks into his eyes, she's stunned to see her soulmate—a vampire whose world she's vowed to destroy.

THE CHOSEN

THE NIGHT WORLD SERIES

• • • • • • • • • • • • • • • • •

Night World

Daughters of Darkness

Spellbinder

Dark Angel

The Chosen

Soulmate

Huntress

Black Dawn

Witchlight

NIGHT WORLD · BOOK FIVE

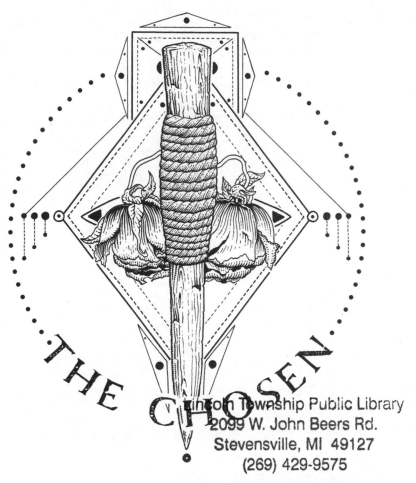

THE CHOSEN

L. J. SMITH

SIMON PULSE

NEW YORK   LONDON   TORONTO   SYDNEY   NEW DELHI

SIMON PULSE

An imprint of Simon & Schuster Children's Publishing Division

1230 Avenue of the Americas, New York, New York 10020

This Simon Pulse hardcover edition April 2017

Text copyright © 1997 by Lisa J. Smith

Cover illustration copyright © 2017 by Neal Williams

Endpaper art of flowers, heart, and sunburst respectively copyright © 2017 by Liliya Shlapak, Nattle, and Ezepov Dmitry/Shutterstock.com

Endpaper art of ornamental flourishes copyright © 2017 by Thinkstock

All rights reserved, including the right of reproduction in whole or in part in any form.

SIMON PULSE and colophon are registered trademarks of Simon & Schuster, Inc.

NIGHT WORLD is a trademark of Lisa J. Smith

For information about special discounts for bulk purchases, please contact Simon & Schuster Special Sales at 1-866-506-1949 or business@simonandschuster.com.

The Simon & Schuster Speakers Bureau can bring authors to your live event.

For more information or to book an event contact the Simon & Schuster Speakers Bureau at 1-866-248-3049 or visit our website at www.simonspeakers.com.

Cover designed by Regina Flath

Interior designed by Mike Rosamilia

The text of this book was set in Adobe Garamond.

Manufactured in the United States of America

2 4 6 8 10 9 7 5 3 1

Library of Congress Control Number 2016948194

ISBN 978-1-4814-8942-3 (hc)

ISBN 978-1-4814-8943-0 (eBook)

For Lolly Carter

CHAPTER 1

It happened at Rashel's birthday party, the day she turned five years old.

"Can we go in the tubes?" She was having her birthday at a carnival and it had the biggest climbing structure of tubes and slides she had ever seen.

Her mother smiled. "Okay, kitten, but take care of Timmy. He's not as fast as you are."

They were the last words her mother ever said to her.

Rashel didn't have to be told, though. She always took care of Timmy: he was a whole month younger than she was, and he wasn't even going to kindergarten next year. He had silky black hair, blue eyes, and a very sweet smile. Rashel had dark hair, too, but her eyes were green—green as emeralds, Mommy always said. Green as a cat's.

As they climbed through the tubes she kept glancing back at him, and when they got to a long row of vinyl-padded stairs—slippery and easy to slide off of—she held out a hand to help him up.

Timmy beamed at her, his tilted blue eyes shining with adoration. When they had both crawled to the top of the stairs, Rashel let go of his hand.

She was heading toward the spiderweb, a big room made entirely of rope and net. Every so often she glanced through a fish-bowl window in one of the tubes and saw her mother waving at her from below. But then another mother came to talk to hers and Rashel stopped looking out. Parents never seemed to be able to talk and wave at the same time.

She concentrated on getting through the tubes, which smelled like plastic with a hint of old socks. She pretended she was a rabbit in a tunnel. And she kept an eye on Timmy—until they got to the base of the spiderweb.

It was far in the back of the climbing structure. There were no other kids around, big or little, and almost no noise. A white rope with knots at regular intervals stretched above Rashel, higher and higher, leading to the web itself.

"Okay, you stay here, and I'll go up and see how you do it," she said to Timmy. This was a sort of fib. The truth was that she didn't think Timmy could make it, and if she waited for him, neither of them would get up.

"No, I don't want you to go without me," Timmy said. There was a touch of anxiety in his voice.

"It's only going to take a second," Rashel said. She knew

what he was afraid of, and she added, "No big kids are going to come and push you."

Timmy still looked doubtful. Rashel said thoughtfully, "Don't you want ice cream cake when we get back to my house?"

It wasn't even a veiled threat. Timmy looked confused, then sighed heavily and nodded. "Okay. I'll wait."

And those were the last words Rashel heard *him* say.

She climbed the rope. It was even harder than she'd thought it would be, but when she got to the top it was wonderful. The whole world was a squiggly moving mass of netting. She had to hang on with both hands to keep her balance and try to curl her feet around the rough quivering lengths of cable. She could feel the air and sunlight. She laughed with exhilaration and bounced, looking at the colored plastic tubes all around her.

When she looked back down for Timmy, he was gone.

Rashel's stomach tensed. He *had* to be there. He'd promised to wait.

But he wasn't. She could see the entire padded room below the spiderweb from here, and it was empty.

Okay, he must have gone back through the tubes. Rashel made her way, staggering and swaying, from one handhold to another until she got to the rope. Then she climbed down quickly and stuck her head in a tube, blinking in the dimness.

"Timmy?" Her voice was a muffled echo. There was no

answer and what she could see of the tube was empty. "Timmy!"

Rashel was getting a very bad feeling in her stomach. In her head, she kept hearing her mother say, *Take care of Timmy.* But she hadn't taken care of him. And he could be anywhere by now, lost in the giant structure, maybe crying, maybe getting shoved around by big kids. Maybe even going to tell her mother.

That was when she saw the gap in the padded room.

It was just big enough for a four-year-old or a very slim five-year-old to get through. A space between two cushiony walls that led to the outside. And Rashel knew immediately that it was where Timmy had gone. It was like him to take the quickest way out. He was probably on his way to her mother right now.

Rashel was a very slim five-year-old. She wiggled through the gap, only sticking once. Then she was outside, breathless in the dusty shade.

She was about to head toward the front of the climbing structure when she noticed the tent flap fluttering.

The tent was made of shiny vinyl and its red and yellow stripes were much brighter than the plastic tubes. The loose flap moved in the breeze and Rashel saw that anyone could just lift it and walk inside.

Timmy wouldn't have gone in *there*, she thought. It wouldn't be like him at all. But somehow Rashel had an odd feeling.

She stared at the flap, hesitating, smelling dust and popcorn in the air. I'm brave, she told herself, and sidled forward. She pushed on the tent beside the flap to widen the gap, and she stretched her neck and peered inside.

It was too dark to see anything, but the smell of popcorn was stronger. Rashel moved farther and farther until she was actually in the tent. And then her eyes adjusted and she realized that she wasn't alone.

There was a tall man in the tent. He was wearing a long light-colored trench coat, even though it was warm outside. He didn't seem to notice Rashel because he had something in his arms, and his head was bent down to it, and he was doing something to it.

And then Rashel saw what he was doing and she knew that the grown-ups had lied when they said ogres and monsters and the things in fairy-tale books weren't real.

Because the tall man had Timmy, and he was *eating* him.

CHAPTER 2

Eating him or doing something with his teeth. Tearing and sucking. Making noises like Pal did when he ate his dog food.

For a moment Rashel was frozen. The whole world had changed and everything seemed like a dream. Then she heard somebody screaming and her throat hurt and she knew it was her.

And then the tall man *looked* at her.

He lifted his head and looked. And she knew that his face alone was going to give her nightmares forever.

Not that he was ugly. But he had hair as red as blood and eyes that shone gold, like an animal's. There was a light in them that was like nothing she had ever seen.

She ran then. It was wrong to leave Timmy, but she was too scared to stay. She wasn't brave; she was a baby, but she couldn't help it. She was still screaming as she turned around and darted through the flap in the tent.

Almost darted through. Her head and shoulders got outside and she saw the red plastic tubes rising above her—and then a hand clamped on the back of her Gymboree shirt. A big strong hand that stopped her in midflight. Rashel was as helpless as a baby kitten against it.

But just as she was dragged back into the tent she saw something. *Her mother.* Her mother was coming around the corner of the climbing structure. She'd heard Rashel screaming.

Her mother's eyes were big and her mouth was open, and she was moving fast. She was coming to save Rashel.

"Mommeeeeeeeee!" Rashel screamed, and then she was back inside the tent. The man threw her to one side the way a kid at preschool would throw a piece of crumpled paper. Rashel landed hard and felt a pain in her leg that normally would have made her cry. Now she hardly noticed it. She was staring at Timmy, who was lying on the ground near her.

Timmy looked strange. His body was like a rag doll's— arms and legs flopped out. His skin was white. His eyes were staring straight up at the top of the tent.

There were two big holes in his throat, with blood all around them.

Rashel whimpered. She was too frightened to scream anymore. But just then she saw white daylight, and a figure in front of it. Mommy. Mommy was pulling the tent flap open. Mommy was inside, looking around for Rashel.

That was when the worst thing happened. The worst and the strangest, the thing the police never believed when Rashel told them later.

Rashel saw her mother's mouth open, saw her mother looking at her, about to say something. And then she heard a voice—but it wasn't Mommy's voice.

And it wasn't an out-loud voice. It was inside her head.

Wait! There's nothing wrong here. But you need to stand very, very still.

Rashel looked at the tall man. His mouth wasn't moving, but the voice was his. Her mother was looking at him, too, and her expression was changing, becoming relaxed and . . . stupid. Mommy was standing very, very still.

Then the tall man hit Mommy once on the side of the neck and she fell over and her head flopped the wrong way like a broken doll. Her dark hair was lying in the dirt.

Rashel saw that and then everything was even more like a dream. Her mother was dead. Timmy was dead. And the man was looking at her.

You're not upset, came the voice in her head. *You're not frightened. You want to come right here.*

Rashel could feel the pull of the voice. It was drawing her closer and closer. It was making her still and not afraid, making her forget her mother. But then she saw the tall man's golden eyes and they were *hungry.* And all of a sudden she remembered what he wanted to do to her.

Not me!

She jerked away from the voice and dove for the tent flap again.

This time she got all the way outside. And she threw herself straight at the gap in the climbing structure.

She was thinking in a different way than she had ever thought before. The Rashel that had watched Mommy fall was locked away in a little room inside her, crying. It was a new Rashel who wiggled desperately through the gap in the padded room, a smart Rashel who knew that there was no point in crying because there was nobody who cared anymore. Mommy couldn't save her, so she had to save herself.

She felt a hand grab her ankle, hard enough almost to crush her bones. It yanked, trying to drag her back through the gap. Rashel kicked backward with all her strength and then twisted, and her sock came off and she pulled her leg into the padded room.

Come back! You need to come back right now!

The voice was like a teacher's voice. It was hard not to listen. But Rashel was already scrambling into the plastic tube in front of her. She went faster than she ever had before, hurting her knees, propelling herself with her bare foot.

When she got to the first fish-bowl window, though, she saw a face looking in at her.

It was the tall man. He was staring at her. He banged on the plastic as she went by.

Fear cracked in Rashel like a belt. She scrambled faster, and the knocks on the tube followed her.

He was underneath her now. Keeping up with her. Rashel passed another window and looked down. She could see his hair shining in the sunlight. She could see his pale face looking up at her.

And his eyes.

Come down, came the voice and it wasn't stern anymore. It was sweet. *Come down and we'll go get some ice cream. What kind of ice cream do you like best?*

Rashel knew then that this was how he'd gotten Timmy into the tent. She didn't even pause in her scrambling.

But she couldn't get away from him. He was traveling with her, just under her, waiting for her to come out or get to a place where he could reach in and grab her.

Higher. I need to get higher, she thought.

She moved instinctively, as if some sixth sense was telling her which way to turn each time she had a choice. She went through angled tubes, straight tubes, tubes that weren't solid at all, but made of woven canvas strips. And finally she got to a place where she couldn't go any higher.

It was a square room with a padded floor and netting sides. She was at the front of the climbing structure; she could see mothers and fathers standing and sitting in little groups. She could feel the wind.

Below her, looking up, was the tall man.

Chocolate brownie? Mint chip? Bubble gum?

The voice was putting pictures in her mind. Tastes. Rashel looked around frantically.

There was so much noise—every kid in the climbing structure was yelling. Who would even notice her if she shouted? They'd think she was joking around.

All you have to do is come down. You know you have to come down sometime.

Rashel looked into the pale face turned up to her. The eyes were like dark holes. Hungry. Patient. Certain.

He knew he was going to get her.

He was going to win. She had no way to fight him.

And then something tore inside Rashel and she did the only thing a five-year-old could do against an adult.

She shoved her hand between the rough cords that made the netting, scraping off skin. She pushed her whole small arm through and she pointed down at the tall man.

And she screamed in a way she'd never screamed before. Piercing shrieks that cut through the happy noise of the other kids. She screamed the way Ms. Bruce at preschool had taught her to do if any stranger ever bothered her.

"Help meeee! Help meeee! That man tried to touch me!"

She kept screaming it, kept pointing. And she saw people look at her.

But they didn't do anything. They just stared. Lots of faces, looking up at her. Nobody moving.

In a way, it was even worse than anything that had happened before. They could hear her, but nobody was going to help her.

And then she saw somebody moving.

It was a big boy, not quite a grown-up man. He was wearing a uniform like the one Rashel's father used to wear before he died. That meant he was a Marine.

He was going toward the tall man, and his face was dark and angry. And now, as if they had only needed this example, other people were moving, too. Several men who looked like fathers. A woman with a cellular phone.

The tall man turned and ran.

He ducked under the climbing structure, heading toward the back, toward the tent where Rashel's mother was. He moved very fast, much faster than any of the people in the crowd.

But he sent words to Rashel's mind before he disappeared completely.

See you later.

When he was definitely gone, Rashel slumped against the netting, feeling the rough cord bite into her cheek. People down below were calling to her; kids just behind her were whispering. None of it really mattered.

She could cry now; it would be okay, but she didn't seem to have any tears.

The police were no good. There were two officers, a man and a woman. The woman believed Rashel a little. But every time her eyes would start to believe, she'd shake her head and say, "But what was the man *really* doing to Timmy? Baby-doll, sweetie, I know it's awful, but just *try* to remember."

The man didn't believe even a little. Rashel would have traded them both for the Marine back at the carnival.

All they'd found in the tent was her mother with a broken neck. No Timmy. Rashel wasn't sure but she thought the man had probably taken him.

She didn't want to think about why.

Eventually the police drove her to her aunt Corinne's, who was the only family she had left now. Aunt Corinne was old and her bony hands hurt Rashel's arms when she clutched her and cried.

She put Rashel in a bedroom full of strange smells and tried to give her medicine to make her sleep. It was like cough syrup, but it made her tongue numb. Rashel waited until Aunt Corinne was gone, then she spat it into her hand and wiped her hand on the sheets, way down at the foot of the bed where the blankets tucked in.

And then she put her arms around her hunched-up knees and sat staring into the darkness.

She was too little, too helpless. That was the problem. She wasn't going to be able to do anything against him when he came back.

Because of course he was coming back.

She knew what the man was, even if the adults didn't

believe her. He was a vampire, just like on TV. A monster that drank blood. And he knew she knew.

That was why he'd promised to see her later.

At last, when Aunt Corinne's house was quiet, Rashel tiptoed to the closet and slid it open. She climbed the shoe rack and squirmed and kicked until she was on the top shelf above the clothes. It was narrow, but wide enough for her. That was one good thing about being little.

She had to use every advantage she had.

With her toe, she slid the closet door back shut. Then she piled sweaters and other folded things from the shelf on top of herself, covering even her head. And finally she curled up on the hard bare wood and shut her eyes.

Sometime in the night she smelled smoke. She got down from the shelf—falling more than climbing—and saw flames in her bedroom.

She never knew exactly how she managed to run through them and get out of the house. The whole night was like one long blurred nightmare.

Because Aunt Corinne didn't get out. When the fire trucks came with their sirens and their flashing lights, it was already too late.

And even though Rashel knew that *he* had set the fire—the vampire—the police didn't believe her. They didn't understand why he had to kill her.

In the morning they took her to a foster home, which

would be the first of many. The people there were nice, but Rashel wouldn't let them hold her or comfort her.

She already knew what she had to do.

If she was going to survive, she had to make herself hard and strong. She couldn't care about anybody else, or trust anybody, or rely on anybody. Nobody could protect her. Not even Mommy had been able to do that.

She had to protect herself. She had to learn to fight.

CHAPTER 3

God, it *stank*.

Rashel Jordan had seen a lot of vampire lairs in her seventeen years, but this was probably the most disgusting. She held her breath as she stirred the nest of tattered cloth with the toe of one boot. She could read the story of this collection of garbage as easily as if the inhabitant had written out a full confession, signed it, and posted it on the wall.

One vampire. A rogue, an outcast who lived on the fringe of both the human world and the Night World. He probably moved to a new city every few weeks to avoid getting caught. And he undoubtedly looked like any other homeless guy, except that none of the human homeless would be hanging around a Boston dock on a Tuesday night in early March.

He brings his victims here, Rashel thought. The pier's deserted, it's private, he can take his time with them. And of course he can't resist keeping a few trophies.

Her foot stirred them gently. A pink-and-blue knit baby jacket, a plaid sash from a school uniform, a Spiderman tennis shoe. All bloodstained. All very small.

There had been a rash of missing children lately. The Boston police would never discover where they had gone—but now Rashel knew. She felt her lips draw back slightly from her teeth in something that wasn't really a smile.

She was aware of everything around her: the soft plash of water against the wooden pier, the rank coppery smell that was almost a taste, the darkness of a night lit only by a half moon. Even the light moisture of the cold breeze against her skin. She was aware of all of it without being preoccupied with any of it— and when the tiny scratch sounded behind her, she moved as smoothly and gracefully as if she were taking her turn in a dance.

She pivoted on her left foot, drawing her *bokken* in the same motion, and without a break in the movement, she stabbed straight to the vampire's chest. She drove the blow from her hips, exhaling in a hiss as she did it, putting all her strength behind it.

"Gotta be faster than that," she said.

The vampire, skewered like a hot dog, waved his arms and gibbered. He was dressed in filthy clothing and his hair was a bushy tangle. His eyes were wide, full of surprise and hatred, shining as silver as an animal's in the faint light. His teeth weren't so much fangs as tusks: fully extended, they reached almost to his chin.

"I know," Rashel said. "You really, really wanted to kill me. Life's tough, isn't it?"

The vampire snarled one more time and then the silver went out of his eyes, leaving only the look of astonishment. His body stiffened and slumped backward. It lay still on the ground.

Grimacing, Rashel pulled her wooden sword out of the chest. She started to wipe the blade on the vampire's pants, then hesitated, peering at them more closely. Yes, those were definitely little crawly things. And the blankets were just as repulsive.

Oh, well. Use your own jeans. It won't be the first time.

She carefully wiped the *bokken* clean. It was two and a half feet long and just slightly, gracefully curved, with a narrow, sharp, angled tip. Designed to penetrate a body as efficiently as possible—if that body was susceptible to wood.

The sword slipped back into its sheath with a papery whisper. Then Rashel glanced at the body again.

Mr. Vampire was already going mummified. His skin was now yellow and tough; his staring eyes were dried up, his lips shrunken, his tusks collapsed.

Rashel bent over him, reaching into her back pocket. What she pulled out looked like the snapped-off end of a bamboo backscratcher—which was exactly what it was. She'd had it for years.

Very precisely, Rashel drew the five lacquered fingers of the scratcher down the vampire's forehead. On the yellow skin five brown marks appeared, like the marks of a cat's claws. Vampire skin was easy to mark right after death.

"This kitten has claws," she murmured. It was a ritual sentence; she'd repeated it ever since the night she'd killed her first vampire at the age of twelve. In memory of her mother, who'd always called her kitten. In memory of herself at age five, and all the innocence she'd lost. She'd never be a helpless kitten again.

Besides, it was a little joke. Vampires . . . bats. Herself . . . a cat. Anybody who'd grown up with Batman and Catwoman would get it.

Well. All done. Whistling softly, she rolled the body over and over with her foot to the end of the pier. She didn't feel like carting the mummy all the way out to the fens, the salt marshes where bodies were traditionally left in Boston. With a mental apology to everybody who was trying to clean up the harbor, she gave the corpse a final push and listened for the splash.

She was still whistling as she emerged from the pier onto the street. *Hi-ho, hi-ho, it's off to work we go.* . . .

She was in a very good mood.

The only disappointment was the constant one, that it hadn't been *the* vampire, the one she'd been looking for ever since she'd been five years old. It had been a rogue, all right— a depraved monster who killed human kids foolishly close to human habitations. But it hadn't been *the* rogue.

Rashel would never forget *his* face. And she knew that someday she would see it again. Meanwhile, there was nothing to do but shish-kebab as many of the parasites as possible.

She scanned the streets as she walked, alert for any sign of Night People. All she saw were quiet brick buildings and streetlights shining pale gold.

And that was a shame, because she was in terrific form tonight; she could feel it. She was every bloodsucking leech's worst enemy. She could stake six of them before breakfast and still be fresh for chemistry first period at Wassaguscus High.

Rashel stopped suddenly, absentmindedly melting into a shadow as a police car cruised silently down the cross-street ahead. *I* know, she thought. I'll go see what the Lancers are up to. If anybody knows where vampires are, they do.

She headed for the North End. Half an hour later she was standing in front of a brownstone apartment building, ringing the buzzer.

"Who's there?"

Instead of answering, Rashel said, "The night has a thousand eyes."

"And the day only one," came the reply from the intercom. "Hey there, girl. Come on up."

Inside, Rashel climbed a dark and narrow stairway to a scarred wooden door. There was a peephole in the door. Rashel faced it squarely, then pulled off the scarf she'd been wearing. It was black, silky, and very long. She wore it wrapped around her head and face like a veil, so that only her eyes showed, and even they were in shadow.

She shook out her hair, knowing what the person on the other side could see. A tall girl dressed like a ninja, all in black, with black hair falling loose around her shoulders and green eyes blazing. She hadn't changed much since she was five, except in height. Right now she made a barbaric face at the peephole and heard the sound of laughter behind the door as bolts were drawn.

She waited until the door was shut behind her again before she said, "Hi, Elliot."

Elliot was a few years older than she was, and thin, with intense eyes and little shiny glasses that were always slipping off his nose. Some people would have dismissed him as a geek. But Rashel had once seen him stand up to two werewolves while she got a human girl out a window, and she knew that he had practically singlehandedly started the Lancers—one of the most successful organizations of vampire hunters on the East Coast.

"What's up, Rashel? It's been a while."

"I've been busy. But now I'm bored. I came to see if you guys had anything going." As Rashel spoke, she was looking at the other people in the room: A brown-haired girl was kneeling, loading objects from boxes into a dark green backpack. Another girl and a boy were sitting on the couch. Rashel recognized the boy from other Lancers meetings, but neither of the girls were familiar.

"Lucky you," Elliot said. "This is Vicky, my new second-in-command." He nodded at the girl on the floor. "She just moved to Boston; she was the leader of a group on the south shore. And tonight she's taking a little expedition out to some warehouses in Mission Hill. We got a lead that there's been some activity out there."

"What kind of activity? Leeches, puppies?"

Elliot shrugged. "Vampires definitely. Werewolves maybe. There's been a rumor about teenage girls getting kidnapped and stashed somewhere around there. The problem is we don't know exactly where, or why." He tilted his head, his eyes twinkling. "You want to go?"

"Isn't anybody going to ask *me*?" Vicky said, straightening up from her backpack. Her pale blue eyes were fixed on Rashel. "I've never even seen this girl before. She could be one of *them*."

Elliot pushed his glasses higher on his nose. He looked amused. "You wouldn't say that if you knew, Vicky. Rashel's the best."

"At what?"

"At everything. When you were going to your fancy prep school, she was out in the Chicago slums staking vampires. She's been in L.A., New York, New Orleans . . . even Vegas. She's wiped out more parasites than the rest of us put together." Elliot glanced mischievously at Rashel, then leaned toward Vicki.

"Ever heard of the Cat?" he said.

Vicki's head snapped up. She stared at Rashel. "The Cat? The one all the Night People are afraid of? The one they're offering a reward for? The one who leaves a mark—"

Rashel shot Elliot a warning look. "Never mind," she said. She wasn't sure she trusted these new people. Vicky was right about one thing: you couldn't be too careful.

And she didn't like Vicky much, but she could hardly turn down such a good opportunity for vampire hunting. Not tonight, when she was in such terrific form.

"I'll go with you—if you'll have me," she said.

Vicky's pale blue eyes bored into Rashel's a moment, then she nodded. "Just remember I'm in charge."

"Sure," Rashel murmured. She could see Elliot's grin out of the corner of her eye.

"You know Steve, and that's Nyala." Elliot indicated the boy and girl on the couch. Steve had blond hair, muscular shoulders, and a steady expression; Nyala had skin like cocoa and a faraway look in her eyes, as if she were sleepwalking. "Nyala's new. She just lost her sister a month ago," Elliot added in a gentle voice. He didn't need to say *how* the sister had been lost.

Rashel nodded at the girl. She sympathized. There was nothing quite like the shock of first discovering the Night World, when you realized that things like vampires and witches and werewolves were real, and that they were *everywhere*, joined in one giant secret organization. That anybody could be one, and you'd never know until it was too late.

"Everybody ready? Then let's go," Vicky said, and Steve and Nyala got up. Elliot showed them to the door.

"Good luck," he said.

Outside, Vicky led the way to a dark blue car with mud strategically caked on the license plates.

"We'll drive to the warehouse area," she said.

Rashel was relieved. She was used to walking the city streets at night without being seen—important when you were carrying a rather unconcealable sword—but she wasn't sure that these other three could manage. It took practice.

The drive was silent except for the murmur of Steve's voice occasionally helping Vicky with directions. They passed through respectable neighborhoods and venerable areas with handsome old buildings until they got to a street where everything changed suddenly. All at once, as if they had crossed some invisible dividing line, the gutters were full of soggy trash and the fences were topped with razor wire. The buildings were government housing projects, dark warehouses, or rowdy bars.

Vicky pulled into a parking lot and stopped the car away from the security lights. Then she led them through the knee-high dead weeds of a vacant lot to a street that was poorly lighted and utterly silent.

"This is the observation post," Vicky whispered, as they reached a squat brick building, a part of the housing project that had been abandoned. Following her, they zigzagged through debris and scrap metal to get to a side door, and then they climbed a dark staircase covered with graffiti to the third floor. Their flashlights provided the only illumination.

"Nice place," Nyala whispered, looking around. She had obviously never seen anything like it before. "Don't you think—there may be other people here besides vampires?"

Steve gave her a reassuring pat. "No, it's okay."

"Yeah, it looks like even the junkies have abandoned it," Rashel said, grimly amused.

"You can see the whole street from the window," Vicky put in shortly. "Elliot and I were here yesterday watching those warehouses across the street. And last night we saw a guy at the end of the street who looked a lot like a vampire. You know the signs."

Nyala opened her mouth as if to say *she* didn't know the signs, but Rashel was already speaking. "Did you test him?"

"We didn't want to get that close. We'll do it tonight if he shows up again."

"How do you test them?" Nyala asked.

Vicky didn't answer. She and Steve had pushed aside a couple of rat-chewed mattresses and were unloading the bags and backpacks they'd brought.

Rashel said, "One way is to shine a flashlight in their eyes. Usually you get eyeshine back—like an animal's."

"There are other ways, too," Vicky said, setting the things she was unloading on the bare boards of the floor. There were ski masks, knives made of both metal and wood, a number of stakes of various sizes, and a mallet. Steve added two clubs made of white oak to the pile.

"Wood hurts them more than metal," Vicky said to Nyala. "If you cut them with a steel knife they heal right before your eyes—but cut them with wood and they keep bleeding."

Rashel didn't quite like the way she said it. And she didn't like the last thing Vicky was pulling out of her backpack. It was a wooden device that looked a bit like a miniature stock. Two hinged blocks of wood that fit snugly around a person's wrists and closed with a lock.

"Vampire handcuffs," Vicky said proudly, seeing her look. "Made of white oak. Guaranteed to hold any parasite. I brought them from down south."

"But hold them for what? And what do you need all those little knives and stakes for? It would take hours to kill a vampire with those."

Vicky smiled fiercely. "I know."

Oh. Rashel's heart seemed to thump and then sink, and she looked away to control her reaction. She understood what Vicky had in mind now.

Torture.

"A quick death's too good for them," Vicky said, still smiling. "They deserve to suffer—the way they make *our* people suffer. Besides, we might get some information. We need to

know where they're keeping the girls they kidnap, and wha
they're doing with them."

"Vicky." Rashel spoke earnestly. "It's practically impossible
to make vampires talk. They're stubborn. When they're hurt
they just get angry—like animals."

Vicky smirked. "I've made some talk. It just depends on
what you do, and how long you make it last. Anyway, there's
no harm in trying."

"Does Elliot know about this?"

Vicky lifted a shoulder defensively. "Elliot lets me do
things my way. I don't have to tell him every little detail. I was
a leader myself, you know."

Helplessly, Rashel looked at Nyala and Steve. And saw
that for the first time Nyala's eyes had lost their sleepwalking
expression. Now she looked awake—and savagely glad.

"*Yes,*" she said. "We should try to make the vampire talk.
And if he suffers—well, my sister suffered. When I found her,
she was almost dead but she could still talk. She told me what
it felt like, having all the blood drained out of her body while
she was still conscious. She said it hurt. She said . . ." Nyala
stopped, swallowed, and looked at Vicky. "I want to help do
it," she said thickly.

Steve didn't say anything, but then from what Rashel knew
of him, that was typical. He was a guy of few words. Anyway,
he didn't protest.

Rashel felt odd, as if she were seeing the very worst of

herself reflected in a mirror. It made her . . . ashamed. It left her shaken.

But who am I to judge? she thought, turning away. It's true that the parasites are evil, all of them. The whole race needs to be wiped out. And Vicky's right, why should they have a clean death, when they usually don't give their victims one? Nyala deserves to avenge her sister.

"Unless you *object* or something," Vicky said heavily, and Rashel could feel those pale blue eyes on her. "Unless you're some kind of vampire sympathizer."

Rashel might have laughed at that, but she wasn't in a laughing mood. She took a breath, then said without turning around, "It's your show. I agreed that you were in charge."

"Good," Vicky said, and returned to her work.

But the sick feeling in the pit of Rashel's stomach didn't go away. She almost hoped that the vampire wouldn't come.

CHAPTER 4

Quinn was cold.

Not physically, of course. That was impossible. The icy March air had no effect on him; his body was impervious to little things like weather. No, this cold was inside him.

He stood looking at the bay and the thriving city across it. Boston by starlight. It had taken him a long time to come back to Boston after . . . the change.

He'd lived there once, when he'd been human. But in those days Boston was nothing but three hills, one beacon, and a handful of houses with thatched roofs. The place where he was standing now had been clean beach surrounded by salt meadows and dense forest.

The year had been 1639.

Boston had grown since then, but Quinn hadn't. He was still eighteen, still the young man who'd loved the sunny pastures and the clear blue water of the wilderness. Who had lived simply, feeling grateful when there was enough food for supper on his mother's table, and who had dreamed of some-day having his own fishing schooner and marrying pretty Dove Redfern.

That was how it had all started, with Dove. Pretty Dove and her soft brown hair . . . sweet Dove, who had a secret a simple boy like Quinn could never have imagined.

Well. Quinn felt his lip curl. That was all in the past. Dove had been dead for centuries, and if her screams still haunted him every night, no one knew but himself.

Because he might not be any older than he had been in the days of the colonies, but he had learned a few tricks. Like how to wrap ice around his heart so that nothing in the world could hurt him. And how to put ice in his gaze, so that whoever looked into his black eyes saw only an end-less glacial dark. He'd gotten very good at that. Some people actually went pale and backed away when he turned his eyes on them.

The tricks had worked for years, allowing him not just to survive as a vampire, but to be brilliantly successful at it. He was Quinn, pitiless as a snake, whose blood ran like ice water, whose soft voice pronounced doom on anybody who got in his way. Quinn, the essence of darkness, who struck fear into the hearts of humans and Night People alike.

And just at the moment, he was tired.

Tired and cold. There was a kind of bleakness inside him, like a winter that would never change into spring.

He had no idea what to do about it—although it had occurred to him that if he were to jump into the bay and let those dark waters close over his head, and then *stay* down there for a few days without feeding . . . well, all his problems would be solved, wouldn't they?

But that was ridiculous. He was Quinn. Nothing could touch him. The bleak feeling would go away eventually.

He pulled himself out of his reverie, turning away from the shimmering blackness of the bay. Maybe he should go to the warehouse in Mission Hill, check on its inhabitants. He needed something to *do*, to keep him from thinking.

Quinn smiled, knowing it was a smile to frighten children. He set off for Boston.

Rashel sat by the window, but not the way ordinary people sit. She was kneeling in a sort of crouch, weight resting on her left leg, right leg bent and pointing forward. It was a position that allowed for swift and unrestricted movement in any direction. Her *bokken* was beside her; she could spring and draw at a second's notice.

The abandoned building was quiet. Steve and Vicky were outside, scouting the street. Nyala seemed lost in her own thoughts.

Suddenly Nyala reached out and touched the *bokken's* sheath. "What's this?"

"Hm? Oh, it's a kind of Japanese sword. They use wooden swords for fencing practice because steel would be too danger-ous. But it can actually be lethal even to humans. It's weighted and balanced just like a steel sword." She pulled the sword out of the sheath and turned the flashlight on it so Nyala could see the satiny green-black wood.

Nyala drew in her breath and touched the graceful curve lightly. "It's beautiful."

"It's made of lignum vitae: the Wood of Life. That's the hardest and heaviest wood there is—it's as dense as iron. I had it carved specially, just for me."

"And you use it to kill vampires."

"Yes."

"And you've killed a lot."

"Yes." Rashel slid the sword back into its sheath.

"Good," Nyala said with a throb in her voice. She turned to stare at the street. She had a small queenly head, with hair piled on the back like Nefertiti's crown. When she turned back to Rashel, her voice was quiet. "How did you get into all this in the first place? I mean, you seem to know so much. How did you learn it all?"

Rashel laughed. "Bit by bit," she said briefly. She didn't like to talk about it. "But I started like you. I saw one of *them* kill my mom when I was five. After that, I tried to learn everything I could about vampires, so I could fight them. And I told the story at every foster home I lived in, and finally

I found some people who believed me. They were vampire hunters. They taught me a lot."

Nyala looked ashamed and disgusted. "I'm so stupid—I haven't done anything like that. I wouldn't even have known about the Lancers if Elliot hadn't called me. He saw the article in the paper about my sister and guessed it might have been a vampire killing. But I'd never have found them on my own."

"You just didn't have enough time."

"No. I think it takes a special kind of person. But now that I know how to fight them, I'm going to do it." Her voice was tight and shaky, and Rashel glanced at her quickly. There was something unstable just under the surface of this girl. "Nobody knows which of them killed my sister, so I just figure I'll get as many of them as I can. I want to—"

"Quiet!" Rashel hissed the word and put a hand over Nyala's mouth at the same instant. Nyala froze.

Rashel sat tensely, listening, then got up like a spring uncoiling and put her head out the window. She listened for another moment, then caught up her scarf and veiled her face with practiced movements. "Grab your ski mask and come on."

"What is it?"

"You're going to get your wish—right now. There's a fight down there. Stay behind me . . . and don't forget your mask."

Nyala didn't need to ask about *that*, she noticed. It was the first thing any vampire hunter learned. If you were recognized and the vampire got away . . . well; it was all over. The Night

People would search until they found you, then strike when you least expected it.

With Nyala behind her, Rashel ran lightly down the stairs and around to the street.

The sounds were coming from a pool of darkness beside one of the warehouses, far from the nearest streetlight. As Rashel reached the place, she could make out the forms of Steve and Vicky, their faces masked, their clubs in their hands. They were struggling with another form.

Oh, for God's sake, Rashel thought, stopping dead.

One other form. The two of them, armed with wood and lying in ambush, couldn't handle one little vampire by themselves? From the racket, she'd thought they must have been surprised by a whole army.

But this vampire seemed to be putting up quite a fight—in fact, he was clearly winning. Throwing his attackers around with supernatural strength, just as if they were ordinary humans and not fearless vampire slayers. He seemed to be enjoying it.

"We've got to help them!" Nyala hissed in Rashel's ear.

"Yeah," Rashel said joylessly. She sighed. "Wait here; I'm going to bonk him on the head."

It wasn't quite that easy. Rashel got behind the vampire without trouble; he was preoccupied with the other two and arrogant enough to be careless. But then she had a problem.

Her *bokken*, the honorable sword of a warrior, had one

purpose: to deliver a clean blow capable of killing instantly. She couldn't bring herself to whack somebody unconscious with it.

It wasn't that she didn't have other weapons. She had plenty—back at home in Marblehead. All the tools of a ninja, and some the ninja had never heard of. And she knew some extremely dirty methods of fighting. She could break bones and crush tendons; she could peel an enemy's trachea out of his neck with her bare hands or drive his ribs into his lungs with her feet.

But those were desperate measures, to be used as a last resort when her own life was at stake and the opposition was overwhelming. She simply couldn't do that to a single enemy when she had the jump on him.

Just then the single enemy threw Steve into a wall, where he landed with a muffled "oof." Rashel felt sorry for him, but it solved her dilemma. She grabbed the oak club Steve had been holding as it rolled across the concrete. Then she circled nimbly as the vampire turned, trying to face her. At that instant Nyala threw herself into the fight, creating a distraction, and Rashel did what she'd said she would. She bonked the vampire on the head, driving the club like a home runner's swing with the force of her hips.

The vampire cried out and fell down motionless.

Rashel raised the club again, watching him. Then she lowered it, looking at Steve and Vicky. "You guys okay?"

Vicky nodded stiffly. She was trying to get her breath. "He surprised us," she said.

Rashel didn't answer. She was very unhappy, and her feeling of being in top form tonight had completely evaporated. This had been the most undignified fight she'd seen in a long while, and . . .

. . . and it bothered her, the way the vampire had cried out as he fell. She couldn't explain why, but it had.

Steve picked himself up. "He shouldn't have been *able* to surprise us," he said. "That was our fault."

Rashel glanced at him. It was true. In this business, you were either ready all the time, expecting the unexpected at any moment, or you were dead.

"He was just good," Vicky said shortly. "Come on, let's get him out of here before somebody sees us. There's a cellar in the other building."

Rashel took hold of the vampire's feet while Steve grabbed his shoulders. He wasn't very big, about Rashel's height and compact. He looked young, about Rashel's age.

Which meant nothing, she reminded herself. A parasite could be a thousand and still look young. They gained eternal life from other people's blood.

She and Steve carried their burden down the stairs into a large dank room that smelled of damp rot and mildew. They dropped him on the cold concrete floor and Rashel straightened to ease her back.

"Okay. Now let's see what he looks like," Vicky said, and turned her flashlight on him.

The vampire was pale, and his black hair looked even blacker against his white skin. His eyelashes were dark on his cheek. A little blood matted his hair in the back.

"I don't think he's the same one Elliot and I saw last night. That one looked bigger," Vicky said.

Nyala pressed forward, staring at her very first captive vampire. "What difference does it make? He's one of them, right? Nobody human could have thrown Steve like that. He might even be the one who killed my sister. And he's ours now." She smiled down, looking almost like someone in love. "You're ours," she said to the unconscious boy on the floor. "Just you wait."

Steve rubbed his shoulder where it had hit the wall. All he said was "Yeah," but his smile wasn't nice.

"I only hope he doesn't die soon," Vicky said, examining the pale face critically. "You hit him pretty hard."

"He's not going to die," Rashel said. "In fact, he'll probably wake up in a few minutes. And we'd better hope he's not one of the really powerful telepaths."

Nyala looked up sharply. "What?"

"Oh—all vampires are telepathic," Rashel said absently. "But there's a big range as to how powerful they are. Most of them can only communicate over a short distance—like within the same house, say. But a few are a lot stronger."

"Even if he *is* strong, it won't matter unless there are other vampires around," Vicky said.

"Which there may be, if you and Elliot saw another one last night."

"Well . . ." Vicky hesitated, then said, "We can check outside, make sure he doesn't have any friends hiding around that warehouse."

Steve was nodding, and Nyala was listening intently. Rashel started to say that from what she'd seen, they couldn't find a vampire in hiding to save their lives—but then she changed her mind.

"Good idea," she said. "You take Nyala and do that. It's better to have three people than two. I'll tie him up before he comes around. I've got bast cord."

Vicky glanced over quickly, but her hostility seemed to have faded since Rashel had knocked the vampire over the head. "Okay, but let's use the handcuffs. Nyala, run up and get them."

Nyala did, and she and Vicky fixed the wooden stocks on the vampire's wrists. Then they left with Steve.

Rashel sat on the floor.

She didn't know what she was doing, or why she'd sent Nyala away. All she knew was that she wanted to be alone, and that she felt . . . rotten.

It wasn't that she didn't have anger. There were times when she got so angry at the universe that it was actually like a little voice inside her whispering, *Kill, kill, kill.* Times when she wanted to strike out blindly, without caring who she hurt.

But just now the little voice was silent, and Rashel felt sick.

To keep herself busy, she tied his feet with bast, a cord made from the inner bark of trees. It was as good for holding a vampire as Vicky's ridiculous handcuffs.

When it was done, she turned the flashlight on him again.

He was good-looking. Clean features that were strongly chiseled but almost delicate. A mouth that at the moment looked rather innocent, but which might be sensuous if he were awake. A body that was lithe and flat-muscled, if not very tall.

All of which had no effect on Rashel. She'd seen attractive vampires before—in fact, an inordinate number of them seemed to be really beautiful. It didn't mean anything. It only stood as a contrast to what they were like inside.

The tall man who'd killed her mother had been handsome. She could still see his face, his golden eyes.

Filthy parasites. Night World scum. They weren't really people. They were monsters.

But they could still feel pain, just like any human. She'd hurt this one when she hit him.

Rashel jumped up and started to pace the cellar.

All right. This vampire deserved to die. They all did. But that didn't mean she had to wait for Vicky to come back and poke him with pointy sticks.

Rashel knew now why she'd sent Nyala away. So she

could give the vampire a clean death. Maybe he didn't deserve it, but she couldn't stand around and watch Vicky kill him slowly. She *couldn't*.

She stopped pacing and went to the unconscious boy.

The flashlight on the floor was still pointing at him, so she could see him clearly. He was wearing a lightweight black shirt—no sweater or coat. Vampires didn't need protection from the cold. Rashel unbuttoned the shirt, exposing his chest. Although the angled tip of her *bokken* could pierce clothing, it was easier to drive it straight into vampire flesh without any barrier in between.

Standing with one foot on either side of the vampire's waist, she drew the heavy wooden sword. She held it with both hands, one near the guard, the other near the knob on the end of the hilt.

She positioned the end exactly over the vampire's heart.

"This kitten has claws," she whispered, hardly aware she was saying it.

Then she took a deep breath, eyes shut. She needed to work to focus, because she'd never done anything like this before. The vampires she'd killed had usually been caught in the middle of some despicable act—and they'd *all* been fighting at the end. She'd never staked one that was lying still.

Concentrate, she thought. You need *zanshin*, continuing mind, awareness of everything without fixing on anything.

She felt her feet becoming part of the cold concrete beneath them, her muscles and bones becoming extensions of the ground. The strike would carry the energy of the earth itself.

Her hands brought the sword up. She was ready for the kill. She opened her eyes to perfect her aim.

And then she saw that the vampire was awake. His eyes were open and he was looking at her.

CHAPTER 5

Rashel froze. Her sword remained in the air, poised over the vampire's heart.

"Well, what are you waiting for?" the vampire said. "Go on and do it."

Rashel didn't know what she was waiting for. The vampire was in a position to block her sword with his wooden handcuffs, but he didn't do any such thing. She could tell by his body language that he wasn't going to, either. Instead he just lay there, looking up at her with eyes that were as dark and empty as the depths of space.

His hair was tousled on his forehead and his mouth was a bleak line. He didn't seem afraid. He just went on staring with those fathomless eyes.

All right, Rashel thought. Do it. Even the leech is telling you to. Do it fast—now.

But instead she found herself pivoting and stepping slowly away from him.

"Sorry," she said out loud. "I don't take orders from parasites."

She kept her sword at the ready in case he made any sudden moves. But all he did was glance down at the wooden handcuffs, wiggle his wrists in them, and then lie back.

"I see," he said with a strange smile. "So it's torture this time, right? Well, that should be amusing for you."

Stake him, dummy, came the little voice in Rashel's head. Don't talk to him. It's dangerous to get in a conversation with his kind.

But she couldn't refocus herself. In a minute, she told the voice. First I have to get my own control back.

She knelt in her ready-for-action crouch and picked up the flashlight, turning it full on his face. He blinked and looked away, squinting.

There. Now she could see him, but he couldn't see her. Vampire eyes were hypersensitive to light. And even if he did manage to get a glimpse of her, she was wearing her scarf. She had all the advantages, and it made her feel more in command of the situation.

"Why would you think we want to torture you?" she said.

He smiled at the ceiling, not trying to look at her. "Because I'm still alive." He raised the handcuffs. "And aren't these traditional? A few vampires from the south shore have turned up mutilated with stocks like these on. It seemed to have been done for fun." Smile.

Vicky's work, Rashel thought. She wished he would stop smiling. It was such a disturbing smile, beautiful and a little mad.

"Unless," the vampire was going on, "it's information you want."

Rashel snorted. "Would I be likely to get information from you if I *did* want it?"

"Well." Smile. "Not likely."

"I didn't think so," Rashel said dryly.

He laughed out loud.

Oh, God, Rashel thought. *Stake* him.

She didn't know what was wrong with her. Okay, he was charming—in a weird way. But she'd known other charming vampires—smooth, practiced flatterers who tried to sweet-talk or cajole their way out of being staked. Some had tried to seduce her. Almost all had tried mind control. It was only because Rashel had the will to resist telepathy that she was alive today.

But this vampire wasn't doing any of the ordinary things— and when he laughed, it made Rashel's heart thump oddly. His whole face changed when he laughed. A sort of light shone in it.

Girl, you are in *trouble*. Kill him quick.

"Look," she said, and she was surprised to find her voice a little shaky. "This isn't personal. And you probably don't care, but I'm not the one who was going to torture you. This is business, and it's what I have to do." She took a deep breath and reached for the sword by her knee.

He turned his face to the light. He wasn't smiling now and there was no amusement in his voice when he said, "I understand. You've got . . . honor." Looking back at the ceiling, he added, "And you're right, this is the way it always has to end when our two races meet. It's kill or be killed. The law of nature."

He was speaking to her as one warrior to another. Suddenly Rashel felt something she'd never felt for a vampire before. Respect. A strange wish that they weren't on opposite sides in this war. A regret that they could never be anything but deadly enemies.

He's somebody I could talk to, she thought. An odd loneliness had taken hold of her. She hadn't realized she cared about having anyone to talk to.

She found herself saying awkwardly, "Is there anybody you want notified—afterward? I mean, do you have any family? I could make sure the news gets around, so they'd know what had happened to you."

She didn't expect him to actually give her any names. That would be crazy. In this game knowledge was power, with each side trying to find out who the players on the other side were. If you could identify someone as a vampire—or a vampire hunter—you knew who to kill.

It was Batman and Catwoman all over. The important thing was to preserve your secret identity.

But this vampire, who was obviously a lunatic, said thoughtfully, "Well, you *could* send a note to my adopted father. He's Hunter Redfern. Sorry I can't give you an address, but he should be somewhere down east." Another smile. "I forgot to tell you my name. It's Quinn."

Rashel felt as if she'd been hit with an oak club.

Quinn.

One of the most dangerous vampires in all the Night World. Maybe *the* most dangerous of the made vampires, the ones who'd started out human. She knew him by reputation—every vampire hunter did. He was supposed to be a deadly fighter and a brilliant strategist; clever, resourceful . . . and cold as ice. He despised humans, held them in utter contempt. He wanted the Night World to wipe them out, except for a few to be used for food.

I was wrong, Rashel thought dazedly. I should have let Vicky torture him. I'm sure he deserves it, if any of them do. God only knows what he's done in his time.

Quinn had turned his head toward her again, looking straight into the flashlight even though it must be hurting his eyes.

"So you see, you'd better kill me fast," he said in a voice soft as snow falling. "Because that's certainly what I'm going to do to *you* if I get loose."

Rashel gave a strained laugh. "Am I supposed to be scared?"

"Only if you have the brains to know who I am." Now he sounded tired and scornful. "Which obviously you don't."

"Well, let me see. I seem to remember *something* about the Redferns. . . . Aren't they the family who controls the vampire part of the Night World Council? The most important family of all the lamia, the born vampires. Descended directly from Maya, the legendary first vampire. And Hunter Redfern is their leader, the upholder of Night World law, the one who colonized America with vampires back in the sixteen hundreds. Tell me if I'm getting any of this wrong."

He gave her a cold glance.

"You see, we have our sources. And I seem to remember them mentioning *your* name, too. You were made a vampire by Hunter . . . and since his own children were all daughters, you're also his heir."

Quinn laughed sourly. "Yes, well, that's an on-again, off-again thing. You might say I have a love-hate relationship with the Redferns. We spend most of the time wishing each other at the bottom of the Atlantic."

"Tch, vampire family infighting," Rashel said. "Why is it always so hard to get along with your folks?" Despite her light words, she had to focus to keep control of her breathing.

It wasn't fear. She truly wasn't scared of him. It was something like confusion. Clearly, she should be killing him at this moment instead of chatting with him. She couldn't understand why she wasn't doing it.

The only excuse she had was that it seemed to make him even more confused and angry than it did her.

"I don't think you've heard *enough* about me," he said, showing his teeth. "I'm your worst nightmare, human. I even shock other vampires. Like old Hunter . . . he has certain ideas about propriety. How you kill, and who. If he knew some of the things I do, he'd fall down dead himself."

Good old Hunter, Rashel thought. The stiff moral patriarch of the Redfern clan, still caught up in the seventeenth century. He might be a vampire, but he was definitely a New Englander.

"Maybe I should find a way to tell him," she said whimsically.

Quinn gave her another cold look, this time tempered with respect. "If I thought you could *find* him, I'd worry."

Rashel was suddenly struck by something. "You know, I don't think I've ever heard anyone say your first name. I mean, I presume you have one."

He blinked. Then, as if he were surprised himself, he said, "John."

"John Quinn. John."

"I didn't invite you to *call* me it."

"All right, whatever." She said it absently, deep in thought. John Quinn. Such a normal name, a *Boston* name. The name of a real person. It made her think of him as a person, instead of as Quinn the Dreadful.

"Look," Rashel said, and then she asked him something she'd never asked a Night Person before. She said, "Did you *want* Hunter Redfern to make you a vampire?"

There was a long pause. Then Quinn said expressionlessly, "As a matter of fact, I wanted to kill him for it."

"I see." I'd want to do the same, Rashel thought. She didn't mean to ask any more questions, but she found herself saying, "Then why did he do it? I mean, why pick you?"

Another pause. Just when she was sure he wouldn't answer, he said, "I was—I wanted to marry one of his daughters. Her name was Dove."

"You wanted to marry a vampire?"

"I didn't know she was a vampire!" This time Quinn's voice was quick and impatient. "Hunter Redfern was accepted in Charlestown. Granted, a few people said his wife had been a witch, but in those days people said that if you smiled in church."

"So he just lived there and nobody knew," Rashel said.

"Most people accepted him." A faint mocking smile curved Quinn's lips. "My own father accepted him, and he was the minister."

Despite herself, Rashel was fascinated. "And you had to be a vampire to marry her? Dove, I mean."

"I didn't get to marry her," Quinn said tonelessly. He seemed as surprised as she was that he was telling her these things. But he went on, seeming to speak almost to himself.

"Hunter wanted me to marry one of his other daughters. I said I'd rather marry a pig. Garnet—that's the oldest—was about as interesting as a stick of wood. And Lily, the middle one, was evil. I could see that in her eyes. I only wanted Dove."

"And you told him that?"

"Of course. He agreed to it finally—and then he told me his family's secret. Well." Quinn laughed bitterly. "He didn't *tell* me, actually. It was more of a demonstration. When I woke up, I was dead and a vampire. It was quite an experience."

Rashel opened her mouth and then shut it again, trying to imagine the horror of it. Finally she just said, "I bet."

They sat for a moment in silence. Rashel had never felt so . . . close to a vampire. Instead of disgust and hatred, she felt pity.

"But what happened to Dove?"

Quinn seemed to tense all over. "She died," he said nastily. It was clear that his confidences were over.

"How?"

"None of your business!"

Rashel tilted her head and looked at him soberly. "How, John Quinn? You know, there are some things you really ought to tell other people. It might help."

"I don't need a damn psychoanalyst," he spat. He was furious now, and there was a dark light in his eyes that ought to have frightened Rashel. He looked as wild as she felt sometimes, when she didn't care who she hurt.

She wasn't frightened. She was strangely calm, the kind of calm she felt when her breathing exercises made her feel one with the earth and absolutely sure of her path.

"Look, Quinn—"

"I really think you'd better kill me now," he said tightly. "Unless you're too stupid or too scared. This wood won't hold forever, you know. And when I get out, I'm going to use that sword on *you.*"

Startled, Rashel looked down at Vicky's handcuffs. They were bent. Not the oak, of course—it was the metal hinges that were coming apart. Soon he'd have enough room to slip them off.

He was very strong, even for a vampire.

And then, with the same odd calm, she realized what she was going to do.

"Yes, that's a good idea," she said. "Keep bending them. I can say that's how you got out."

"What are you talking about?"

Rashel got up and searched for a steel knife to cut the cords on his feet. "I'm letting you go, John Quinn," she said.

He paused in his wrenching of the handcuffs. "You're insane," he said, as if he'd just discovered this.

"You may be right." Rashel found the knife and slit through the bast cords.

He gave the handcuffs a twist. "If," he said deliberately, "you think that because I was a human once, I have any pity on them, you are very, very wrong. I hate humans more than I hate the Redferns."

"Why?"

He bared his teeth. "No, thank you. I don't have to explain anything to you. Just take my word for it."

She believed him. He looked as angry and as dangerous as an animal in a trap. "All right," she said, stepping back and putting her hand on the hilt of her *bokken.* "Take your best shot. But remember, I beat you once. I was the one who knocked you out."

He blinked. Then he shook his head in disbelief. "You little *idiot,*" he said. "I wasn't paying attention. I thought you were another of those jerks falling over their own feet. And I wasn't even fighting *them* seriously." He sat up in one fluid motion that showed the strength he had, and the control of his own body.

"You don't have a chance," he said softly, turning those dark eyes on her. Now that he wasn't looking into the flashlight, his pupils were huge. "You're dead already."

Rashel had a sinking feeling that was telling her the same thing.

"I'm faster than any human," the soft voice went on. "I'm stronger than any human. I can see better in the dark. And I'm much, much nastier."

Panic exploded inside Rashel.

All at once, she believed him absolutely. She couldn't seem

to get her breath, and a void had opened in her stomach. She lost any vestige of her previous calm.

He's right—you were an idiot, she told herself wildly. You had every chance to stop him and you blew it. And why? Because you were sorry for him? Sorry for a deranged monster who's going to tear you limb from limb now? Anyone as stupid as that *deserves* what they get.

She felt as if she were falling, unable to get hold of anything. . . .

And then suddenly she did seem to catch something. Something that she clung to desperately, trying to resist the fear that wanted to suck her into darkness.

You couldn't have done anything else.

It was the little voice in her mind, being helpful for once. And, strangely, Rashel knew it was true. She *couldn't* have killed him when he was tied up and helpless, not without becoming a monster herself. And after hearing his story, she couldn't have ignored the pity she felt.

I'm probably going to die now, she thought. And I'm still scared. But I'd do it over again. It was right.

She hung on to that as she let the last seconds tick away, the last window of opportunity to stake him while the cuffs still held. She knew they were ticking away, and she knew Quinn knew.

"What a shame to rip your throat out," he said.

Rashel held her ground.

Quinn gave the handcuffs a final wrench, and the metal hinges squealed. Then the stocks clattered onto the concrete and he stood up, free. Rashel couldn't see his face anymore; it was above the reach of the flashlight.

"Well," he said evenly.

Rashel whispered, "Well."

They stood facing each other.

Rashel was waiting for the tiny involuntary body movements that would give away which direction he was going to lunge. But he was more still than any enemy she'd ever seen. He kept his tension inside, ready to explode only when he directed it. His control seemed to be complete.

He's got *zanshin*, she thought.

"You're very good," she said softly.

"Thanks. So are you."

"Thanks."

"But it isn't going to matter in the end."

Rashel started to say, "We'll see"—and he lunged.

She had an instant's warning. A barely perceptible movement of his leg told her he was going to spring to his right, her left. Her body reacted without her direction, moving smoothly . . . and she didn't realize until she was doing it that she wasn't using the sword.

She had stepped forward, inside his attack, and deflected it with a mirror palm block, striking the inner side of his arm with her left arm. Hitting the nerves to try and numb the limb.

But not cutting him. She realized with a dizzy sense of horror that she didn't *want* to use the sword on him.

"You are going to *die*, idiot," he told her, and for an instant she wasn't sure if it was him saying it or the voice in her head.

She tried to push him away. All she could think was that she needed time, time to get her survival reflexes back. She shoved at him—

—and then her bare hand brushed his, and something happened that was completely beyond her experience.

CHAPTER 6

What she felt was a shivering jolt that began in her palm and ran up her arm like electricity. It left tingling in its wake. But the real shock was in her head.

Her mind exploded. That was the only way she could describe it. A noiseless, heatless explosion that shattered her completely. All at once, Rashel couldn't support her own weight anymore. She could feel Quinn's arms supporting her.

She had no sense of the room around her. She was floating in a white light and the only solid thing to hang on to was Quinn. It was something like the terror she'd felt before . . . but it wasn't just terror. Impossibly, what she felt was more like wild elation.

She realized that Quinn was holding her so tightly that it hurt. But even stronger than the sensation of his arms was the sense she had of his *mind.* A direct conduit seemed to have opened between them. She could feel his astonishment, his shock, his wonder. And she knew he could feel hers.

It's telepathy, some distant part of herself said, trying desperately to get control again. It's some new vampire trick.

But she knew it wasn't a trick. Quinn was as astounded as she was—she could *feel* that. Maybe he was even worse off. He was breathing rapidly and shallowly and a fine trembling seemed to have taken over his body.

Rashel held on to him, thinking crazy things. She wanted to comfort him. She could sense, probably better than he could himself, how frighteningly vulnerable he was under that frozen exterior.

Like me, I suppose, Rashel thought giddily. And then she suddenly realized that *he* was feeling *her* vulnerability just as she had felt his. Fear welled up in her so sharply that she panicked.

She tried to find a way to shut him out, to resist the way she resisted mind control—but she knew it was useless. He had gotten past her guard already. He was *inside*.

"It's all right," Quinn said, and she realized that he had stopped trembling. His voice was almost dispassionate, and at the same time madly gentle. Rashel had the feeling that he'd decided that since he couldn't fight this thing, he might as well be as insane as possible.

Strangest of all, she found his words reassuring.

And there was fire under the ice that seemed to encase

him. She could feel that now, and she had the dizzy sense that she was the first one to discover it.

They had fallen to the floor somehow, and they were sitting just at the edge of the light. Quinn was holding her by the shoulders, precisely, and Rashel was astonished at her own response to the clinical grip. It stopped her breath, held her absolutely motionless.

Then, just as precisely, every movement deliberate, Quinn found the end of her scarf and began to unwind it.

He was still filled with that mad gentleness, that lunatic calm. And she wasn't stopping him. He was going to expose her face, and she wasn't doing a thing about it.

She *wanted* him to. In spite of her terror, she wanted him to see her, to know who she was. She wanted to be face-to-face with him in that strange light that had enveloped both their minds. It didn't seem to matter what happened afterward.

She said, "John."

He unwound another length of the scarf, preoccupied and intent as if he were making some archaeological discovery. "You didn't tell me your name." It was a statement. He wasn't pushing her.

She might as well write it out on a death warrant and hand it to him. Quinn could reveal himself to humans—but then Quinn could disappear completely if he wanted, hole up in some hidden vampire enclave where no human could search him out. Rashel couldn't. He knew she was a vampire hunter.

If he knew her name and her face, he'd have every power to destroy her.

And the scariest thing of all was that some part of her didn't care.

He was down to the last turn of the scarf. In a moment her face would be exposed to the air . . . and to vampire eyes that could see in this darkness.

I'm Rashel, Rashel thought. She couldn't quite get the words to her lips. She took a deep breath.

And at the same instant a light blazed into her eyes.

Not the ghostly light that had been in her mind. Real light, the beams from several high-power flashlights, harsh and horribly bright. They cut through the dark cellar and threw Rashel and Quinn into stark illumination.

Rashel gasped. One hand instinctively flew to her scarf to keep it over her face. She felt as if she had been caught naked.

And she was horrified to realize that she hadn't heard anyone come into the cellar. She had been completely absorbed, oblivious to her surroundings. What had happened to all her training? What was *wrong* with her?

She couldn't see anything beyond the light. Her first thought was that it was Quinn's vampire friends come to save him. He seemed to think it might be, too; at least he was standing shoulder to shoulder with her, even trying to push her back a little.

With an odd pang, Rashel realized she could only guess

what he was thinking now. The connection between them had been cleanly severed.

Then a voice came from beyond the terrible brightness, a sharp voice filled with outrage. "How did he get loose? What are you two *doing*?"

Vicky. I'm going insane, Rashel thought. I completely forgot about her and the others coming back. No, I forgot about their existence.

But there were more than three flashlights on the stairs.

"The Big E sent us some backup," Vicky was saying, and Rashel felt a surge of fear. She counted five flashlights, and in the edges of beams she caught the figures of a couple of sturdy-looking guys. Lancers.

Rashel tried desperately to gather her wits.

She knew what had to be done, at least. She nudged Quinn with her shoulder and whispered, "Get out of here. There should be another stairway on the other side of the room. When you run for it, I'll get in their way." She pitched her voice so low that only vampire ears could hear it. The good thing about having her face veiled was that nobody could read her lips.

But Quinn wasn't going. He looked as if he'd just been awakened with a bucketful of ice water. Shocked, angry, and still a little dazed. He stood where he was, staring into all the flashlights like an animal at bay.

The lights were advancing. Rashel could make out Vicky's

figure now at the front. There was going to be a fight, and people were going to get killed.

Steve's voice said, "What did he do to you?"

"What's she been doing with *him*, that's the question," Vicky snapped back. Then she said clearly, "Remember, everybody, we want him alive."

Rashel gave Quinn a harder shove. *"Go."* When he just glared, she hissed, "Don't you realize what they want to do to you?"

Quinn turned so that the advancing party couldn't see his face. He snarled, "They're not exactly overjoyed with *you* either."

"I can take care of myself." Rashel was shaking with frustration. "Just leave. Go!"

Quinn looked as angry with her as he was with the hunters. He didn't want her help, she realized. He wasn't used to taking anything from anyone, and to be forced to do it made him furious.

But there wasn't any other choice. And Quinn finally seemed to recognize that. With one last glare at her, he broke and headed for the darkness at the other side of the cellar.

The flashlights swung in confusion. Rashel, glad to be able to *move*, sprang between the vampire hunters and the stairway.

And then there was a lot of fumbling and crashing, with people running into each other and swearing and yelling.

Rashel enjoyed the chance to work off her frustration. She got in everyone's way long enough for a very fast vampire to disappear.

After which it was just her and the vampire hunters. Five flashlights turned on her and seven amazed and angry people staring.

Rashel got up and brushed herself off. Time to face the consequences. She stood, head high, looking at all of them.

"What happened?" Steve said. "Did he hypnotize you?"

Good old Steve. Rashel felt a rush of warmth toward him. But she couldn't use the out he was offering her. She said, "I don't know what happened."

And *that* was true. She couldn't even begin to explain to herself what had gone on between her and the vampire. She'd never heard of anything like it.

"I think you let him get away on purpose," Vicky said. Rashel couldn't see Vicky's pale blue eyes, but she sensed that they were as hard as marbles. "I think you planned it from the beginning—that's why you told us to go up to the street."

"Is that true?" One of the flashlights swung down and suddenly Nyala was in front of Rashel, her body tense, her voice almost pleading. Her eyes were fixed on Rashel's, begging Rashel to say it wasn't so. "Did you do it on purpose?"

All at once Rashel felt very tired. Nyala was fragile and unstable, and in her own mind she'd made Rashel into a hero. Now that image was being shattered.

For Nyala's sake, Rashel almost wished she could lie. But that would be worse in the end. She said expressionlessly, "Yes. I did it on purpose."

Nyala recoiled as if Rashel had slapped her.

I don't blame you, Rashel thought. I think it's crazy, too.

The truth was that the farther away she got from Quinn's presence, the less she could understand what she'd done. It was beginning to seem like a dream, and not a very clear dream at that.

"But *why?*" one of the Lancer boys at the back asked. The Lancers knew Rashel, knew her reputation. They didn't want to think the worst of her. Like Nyala, they desperately wanted an excuse.

"I don't know why," Rashel said, looking away. "But he wasn't controlling my mind."

Nyala exploded.

"I *hate* you," she burst out. She was trembling with fury, spitting out sentences at Rashel like poison darts. "That vampire could have been the one who killed my sister. Or he could have known who did it. I was going to ask him that, but now I'll never get the chance. Because of *you*. You let him go. We had him and you let him go!"

"It's more than that," Vicky put in, her voice cold and contemptuous. "We were going to ask him about those teenage girls getting kidnapped. Now we can't. So it's going to keep happening, and it's all going to be your fault."

And they were right. Even Nyala was right. How did Rashel know that Quinn hadn't killed Nyala's sister?

"You're a vampire lover," Vicky was saying. "I could tell from the beginning. I don't know, maybe you're one of those damned Daybreakers who wants us all to get along, but you're not on *our* side."

A couple of the Lancers started to protest at this, but Nyala's voice cut through them. "She's on *their* side?" She stared from Vicky to Rashel, her body rigid. "You just wait. Just wait until I tell people that Rashel is the Cat and that she's really on the Night World side. *You just wait.*"

She's hysterical, Rashel realized. Even Vicky was looking surprised at this, as if she were uneasy at what she'd started.

"Nyala, listen—" Rashel began.

But Nyala seemed to have reached some peak of fury at which nothing from outside could touch her. "I'll tell everybody in Boston! You'll see!" She whirled around and plunged toward the stairway as if she were going to start doing it right now.

Rashel stared after her. Then she said to Vicky, "You'd better send a couple of the guys to catch up to her. She's not safe alone in this neighborhood."

Vicky gave her a look that was half angry and half shaken. "Yeah. Okay. Everybody but Steve go after her. You guys take her home."

They left, not without a few backward glances at Rashel.

"We'll drive you back," Vicky said. Her voice wasn't warm, but it wasn't as hostile as it had been.

"I'll walk to my own car," Rashel said flatly.

"Fine." Vicky hesitated, then blurted, "She probably won't do what she said. She's just upset."

Rashel said nothing. Nyala had sounded—and looked—as if she meant to do *exactly* what she said. And if she did . . .

Well, it would be an interesting question as to who would kill Rashel first, the vampires or the vampire hunters.

Wednesday morning dawned with gray skies and icy rain. Rashel trudged from class to class at Wassaguscus High, lost in thought. At home, her latest foster family left her alone—they were used to her going her own way. She sat in her small bedroom in the townhouse with the lights dimmed, thinking.

She still couldn't understand what had happened to her, but with every hour the memory of it was fading steadily. It was too *strange* to fit into the reality of life, and it became more and more like a dream. One of those dreams in which you do things you would never ordinarily do, and are ashamed of when you wake up in the morning.

All that warmth and closeness—she'd felt that for a *vampire*? She'd been excited by a parasite's touch? She'd wanted to comfort a leech?

And not just any leech, either. The infamous Quinn. The

legendary human hater. How could she have let him go? How many people would suffer because of her lapse in sanity?

Who knows, she decided finally, maybe it *had* been some kind of mind control. She certainly couldn't make any sense of it otherwise.

By Thursday, one thing at least was clear in her mind. Vicky had been right about the consequences of what she'd done. Rashel hadn't thought about that at the time, but now she had to face it. She had to make it right.

She had to find the kidnapped girls on her own—if girls *were* getting kidnapped. There was nothing about missing teenagers in the *Globe*. But if it was happening, Rashel had to find out about it and stop it . . . if she could.

Okay. So she'd go back to Mission Hill tonight and start investigating. Check the warehouse area again—this time, her way.

There was one other thing that was clear to her, that became obvious as she got her priorities straight. Something she had to do, not for Nyala, or for Vicky, or for the Lancers, but just for herself. For her own honor, and for everybody who lived in the world of sunlight.

The next time she saw Quinn, she had to kill him.

Rashel moved along the deserted street, keeping to the shadows, moving silently. Not easy when the ground was wet and strewn with broken glass. There were no sidewalks, no grass, no plant life of any kind except the dead weeds in the abandoned lots. Just soggy trash and shattered bottles.

A grim place. It fit Rashel's mood as she made her way stealthily toward the abandoned project building where Vicky had brought them Tuesday night.

From its front door, she surveyed the rest of the street. Lots of warehouses. Several of them were protected with high chain-link fences topped with barbed wire. All of them had barred windows—or no windows—and metal freight doors.

The security precautions didn't bother Rashel. She knew how to cut chain-link and pick locks. What bothered her was that she didn't know where to start.

The Night People could be using any of the warehouses. Even knowing where Steve and Vicky had fought Quinn didn't help, because *he* had jumped *them*. He'd obviously seen them lying in ambush and deliberately gone after them. Which meant his real destination could have been any of the buildings on this street—or none of them.

All right. Patience was indicated here. She'd just have to start at one end . . .

Rashel lost her thought and leaped back into the shadows before she consciously realized why she was doing it. Her ears had picked up a sound—a low rumbling coming from somewhere across the street.

She flattened herself against the brick wall behind her, then kept her body absolutely immobile. Her eyes darted from building to building and she held her breath to hear better.

There. It was coming from inside *that* warehouse, the one down at the far end of the street. And she could identify it now—the sound of an engine.

As she watched, the freight door in the front of the warehouse went sliding up. Headlights pierced the night from behind it. A truck was pulling out onto the street.

Not a very big truck. A U-Haul. It cleared the doors and stopped. A figure was pulling the sliding metal door down. Now it was making its way to the cab of the U-Haul, climbing in.

Rashel strained her eyes, trying to make out any signs of vampirism in the figure's movements. She thought she could detect a certain telltale fluidity to the walk, but it was too far away to be sure. And there was nothing else to give her a clue about what was going on.

It could be a human, she thought. Some warehouse owner going home after a night of balancing books.

But her instinct told her differently. The hair at the back of her neck was standing on end.

And then, as the truck began to cruise off, something happened that settled her doubts and sent her flying down the street.

The back doors of the U-Haul opened just a bit, and a girl fell out. She was slender, and a streetlight caught her blond hair. She landed on the rubble-strewn road and lay there for an instant as if dazed. Then she jumped up, looked around wildly, and started running in Rashel's direction.

CHAPTER 7

By the time Rashel intercepted the girl, the truck was already braking to turn around. Someone was shouting, "She's out! We lost one!"

"This way!" Rashel said, reaching toward the girl with one hand and gesturing with the other.

Up close, she could see that the girl was small, with disheveled blond hair falling over her forehead. Her chest was heaving. Instead of looking grateful, she seemed terrified by Rashel's arrival. She stared at Rashel a moment, then she tried to dart away.

Rashel snagged her in midlunge. "I'm your friend! Come on! We've got to go *between* streets, where the truck can't follow us."

The truck was finishing its turn. Headlights swept toward them. Rashel looped an arm around the girl's waist and took off at a dead run.

The blond girl was carried along. She whimpered but she ran, too.

Rashel was heading for the area between two of the warehouses. She knew that if there really were vampires in that truck, her only chance was to get herself and the blond girl to her car. The vampires could run much faster than any human.

She'd picked these two warehouses because the chain-link fence behind them wasn't too high and had no barbed wire at the top. As they reached it, Rashel gave the girl a little shove. "Climb!"

"I can't!" The girl was trembling and gasping. Rashel looked her over and realized that it was probably the literal truth. The girl didn't look as if she'd ever climbed anything in her life. She was wearing what seemed to be party clothes and high heels.

Rashel saw the truck's headlights in the street and heard the engine slowing.

"You have to!" she said. "Unless you want to go back with *them*." She interlocked her fingers, making a step with her hands. "Here! Put your foot here and then just try to grab on when I bounce you up."

The girl looked too scared not to try. She put her foot in Rashel's hand—just as the headlights switched off.

It was what Rashel had expected. The darkness was an advantage to the vampires; they could see much better in it than humans. They were going to follow on foot.

Rashel took a breath, then heaved upward explosively as

she exhaled. The blond girl went sailing toward the top of the
fence with a shriek.

A bare instant later, Rashel launched herself at the top of
the fence, grabbed it, and swung her legs over. She dropped
to the ground almost noiselessly and held her arms up to the
blond girl.

"Let go! I'll catch you."

The girl, who was clambering awkwardly over the top,
looked over her shoulder. "I can't—"

"Do it!"

The girl dropped. Rashel broke her fall, set her on her feet,
and grabbed her arm above the elbow. "Come on!"

As they ran, Rashel scanned the buildings around them.
She needed a corner, someplace where she could get the girl
behind her and safe. She could defend a corner—if there
weren't more than two or three vampires.

"How many of them are there?" she asked the girl.

"Huh?" The girl was gasping.

"How—many—are—there?"

"I don't know, and I can't run anymore!" The girl staggered
to a halt and bent double, hands on her knees, trying to get her
breath back. "My legs . . . are just like jelly."

It was no use, Rashel realized in dismay. She couldn't
expect this bit of blond fluff to outsprint a vampire. But if they
stopped here in the open, they were dead. She cast a desperate
look around.

Then she saw it. A Bostonian tradition—an abandoned car. In this city, if you got tired of your car you just junked it on the nearest embankment. Rashel blessed the unknown benefactor who'd left this one. Now, if only they could get in. . . .

"This way!" She didn't wait for the girl to protest, but grabbed her and dragged her. "Come on, you can do it! Make it to that car and you don't have to run anymore."

The words seemed to inspire the girl into a last effort. They reached the car and Rashel saw that one of the back windows was broken out cleanly.

"In!"

The girl was small-boned and went through the window easily. Rashel dove after her. Then she shoved her down into the leg space in front of the seat and hissed, "Don't make a sound."

She lay tensely, listening. She barely had time to breathe twice before she heard footsteps.

Soft footsteps, stealthy as a prowling tiger's. Vampire footsteps. Rashel held her breath and waited.

Closer, closer . . . Rashel could feel the other girl shaking. She watched the dark ceiling of the car and tried to plan a defense if they were caught.

The footsteps were right outside now. She heard the grate of glass not ten feet from the car door.

Just please don't let them have a werewolf with them, she thought. Vampires might see and hear better than humans, but a werewolf could sniff its prey out. It couldn't possibly miss the smell of humans in the car.

Outside, the footsteps paused, and Rashel's heart sank. Eyes open, she silently put her hand on her sword.

And then she heard the footsteps moving quickly—away. She listened as they faded, keeping utterly still. Then she kept still some more, while she counted to two hundred.

Then, very carefully, she sat up and looked around.

No sight or sound of vampires.

"Can I *please* get up now?" came a small whimpering voice from the floor.

"If you keep quiet," Rashel whispered. "They still may be somewhere nearby. We're going to have to get to my car without them catching us."

"Anything, as long as I don't have to *run*," the girl said plaintively, emerging from the floor more disheveled than ever. "Have you ever tried to run in four-inch heels?"

"I never wear heels," Rashel murmured, scanning up and down the street. "Okay, I'll get out first, then you come through."

She slid out the window feet-first. The girl stuck her head through. "Don't you ever use *doors*?"

"Shh. Come on," Rashel whispered. She led the way through the dark streets, moving from shadow to shadow. At least the girl could walk softly, she thought. And she had a sense of humor even in danger. That was rare.

Rashel drew a breath of relief when they reached the narrow twisting alley where her Saturn was parked. They weren't safe yet, though. She wanted to get the blond girl out of Mission Hill.

"Where do you live?" she said, as she started the engine. When there was no answer, she turned. The girl was staring at her with open uneasiness.

"Uh, how come you're dressed like that? And who are you, anyway? I mean, I'm glad you saved me—but I don't understand *anything*."

Rashel hesitated. She needed information from this girl, and that was going to take time—and trust. With sudden decision she unwound her scarf, one-handed, until her face was exposed. "Like I said, I'm a friend. But first just tell me: do you know what kind of people had you in that truck?"

The girl turned away. She was already shivering with cold; now she shivered harder. "They weren't people. They were . . . ugh."

"Then you do know. Well, I'm one of the people that hunts down *that* kind of people."

The girl looked from Rashel's face to the sheathed sword that rested between them. Her jaw dropped. "Oh, my God! You're Buffy the Vampire Slayer!"

"Huh? Oh." Rashel had missed the movie. "Right. Actually, you can call me Rashel. And you're . . . ?"

"Daphne Childs. And I live in Somerville, but I don't want to go home."

"Well, that's fine, because I want to talk to you. Let's find a Dunkin' Donuts."

Rashel found one outside of Boston, a safe one she knew had no Night World connections. She pulled a coat on over her black ninja outfit and lent Daphne a spare sweater from the trunk of her car. Then they went inside and ordered jelly sticks and hot chocolate.

"Now," Rashel said. "Tell me what happened. How did you end up in that truck?"

Daphne cupped her hands around her hot chocolate. "It was all so *horrible.* . . ."

"I know." Rashel tried to make her voice soothing. She hadn't had much practice at it. "Try to tell me anyway. Start at the beginning."

"Okay, well, it started at the Crypt."

"Uh, as in *Tales from the* . . . ? Or as in the Old Burial Ground?"

"As in the club on Prentiss Street. It's this underground club, and I mean *really* underground. I mean, nobody seems to know about it except the people who go there, and they're all our age. Sixteen or seventeen. I never see any adults, not even DJs."

"Go on." Rashel was listening intently. The Night People had clubs, usually carefully hidden from humans. Could Daphne have wandered into one?

"Well. It's *extremely* and seriously cool—or at least that's what I thought. They have some amazing music. I mean, it's beyond doom, it's beyond goth, it's sort of like *void* rock. Just listening to it makes you go all weird and bodiless. And the whole place is decorated like this post-apocalypse wasteland. Or maybe like the underworld. . . ." Daphne stared off into the distance. Her eyes, a very deep cornflower blue under heavy lashes, looked wistful and almost hypnotized.

Rashel poked her and chocolate slopped onto the table. "Reminisce about it later. What kind of people were in the club? Vampires?"

"Oh, no." Daphne looked shocked. "Just regular kids. I know some from my school. And there's lots of runaways, I guess. Street kids, you know."

Rashel blinked. "Runaways . . ."

"Yeah. They're mostly very cool, except the ones who do drugs. Those are spooky."

An illegal club full of runaway kids, some of whom would probably do anything for drugs. Rashel could feel her skin tingling.

I think I've stumbled onto something big.

"Anyway," Daphne was going on, "I'd been going there for about three weeks, you know, whenever I could get away from home—"

"You didn't tell your parents about it," Rashel guessed flatly.

"Are you joking? It's not a place you tell *parents* about.

Anyway, my family doesn't care where I go. I've got four sisters and two brothers and my mom and my stepdad are getting divorced . . . they don't even notice when I'm gone."

"Go on," Rashel said grimly.

"Well, there was this guy." Daphne's cornflower eyes looked wistful again. "This guy who was really gorgeous, and really mysterious, and really just—just *different* from anybody I ever met. And I thought he was maybe interested in me, because I saw him looking at me once or twice, so I sort of joined the girls who were always hanging around him. We used to talk about weird things."

"Like?"

"Oh, like surrendering yourself to the darkness and stuff. It was like the music, you know—we were all really into death. Like what would be the most horrible way to die, what would be the most awful torture you could live through, what you look like when you're in your grave. Stuff like that."

"For God's sake, *why*?" Rashel couldn't disguise her revulsion.

"I don't know." All at once, Daphne looked small and sad. "I guess because most of us felt life was pretty rotten. So you kind of face things, you know, to try to get used to them. You probably don't understand," she added, grimacing.

Rashel did understand. With a sudden shock, she understood completely. These kids were scared and depressed and worried about the future. They had to do something to deaden the pain . . . even if that meant embracing pain. They escaped one darkness by going into another.

And am I any different? I mean, this obsession I've got with vampires . . . it's not exactly what you'd call normal and healthy. I spend my whole life dealing with death.

"I'm sorry," she said, and her voice came out more gentle than when she'd been trying to soothe Daphne before. Awkwardly, she patted the other girl's arm once. "I shouldn't have yelled. And I do understand, actually. Please go on."

"Well." Daphne still looked defensive. "Some of the girls would write poetry about dying . . . and some of them would prick themselves with pins and lick the blood off. They said they were vampires, you know. Just pretending." She glanced warily at Rashel.

Rashel simply nodded.

"And so I talked the same way, and did the same stuff. And this guy Quinn just seemed to love it—hey, look out!" Daphne jerked back to avoid a wave of hot chocolate. Rashel's sudden movement had knocked her cup over.

Oh, God, what is wrong *with me?* Rashel thought. She said, "Sorry," through her teeth, grabbing for a wad of napkins.

She should have been expecting it. She *had* been expecting it; she knew that Quinn must be involved in this. But somehow the mention of his name had knocked the props from under her. She hadn't been able to control her reaction.

"So," she said, still through her teeth, "the gorgeous mysterious guy was named Quinn."

"Yeah." Daphne wiped chocolate off her arm. "And I was starting to think he really liked me. He told me to come to the club last Sunday and to meet him alone in the parking lot."

"And you did." Oh, I am going to kill him so dead, Rashel thought.

"Sure. I dressed up . . ." Daphne looked down at her bedraggled outfit. "Well, this *did* look terrific once. So I met him and we went to his car. And then he told me that he'd chosen me. I was so happy I almost fainted. I thought he meant for his girlfriend. And then . . ." Daphne trailed off again. For the first time since she'd begun the story, she looked frightened. "Then he asked me if I really wanted to surrender to the darkness. He made it sound so romantic."

"I bet," Rashel said. She rested her head on her hand. She could see it all now, and it was the perfect scam. Quinn checked the girls out, discovered which would be missed and which wouldn't. He kidnapped them from the parking lot so that no one saw them, no one even connected them with the Crypt. Who would notice or care that certain girls stopped showing up? Girls would always be coming and going.

And there had been nothing in the newspaper because the daylight world didn't realize that girls were being taken. There probably wasn't even a struggle during the abduction, because these girls were *willing* to go—in the beginning.

"It must have been a shock," Rashel said dryly, "to find out that there really *was* a darkness to surrender to."

"Uh, yeah. Yeah, it was. But I didn't actually find that out then. I just said, sure, I wanted to. I mean, I'd have said the same thing if he asked me did I really want to watch Lawrence Welk reruns with him. He was that gorgeous. And he was looking at me in this totally *soulful* way, and I thought he was going to kiss me. And then . . . I fell asleep." Daphne frowned at her paper cup.

"No, you didn't."

"I *did*. I know it sounds crazy, but I fell asleep and when I woke up I was in this place, this little office in this warehouse. And I was on this iron cot with this pathetic lumpy mattress, and I was *chained down*. I had *chains* on my ankles, just like people in jail. And Quinn was gone, and there were two other girls chained to other cots." Without warning, Daphne began to cry.

Rashel handed her a napkin, feeling uncomfortable. "Were the girls from the Crypt, too?"

Daphne sniffed. "I don't know. They might have been. But they wouldn't *talk* to me. They were, like, in a trance. They just lay there and stared at the ceiling."

"But you weren't in a trance," Rashel said thoughtfully. "Somehow you woke up from the mind control. You must be resistant like me."

"I don't know anything about mind control. But I was so

scared I pretended to be like the other girls when this guy came to bring us food and take us to the bathroom. I just stared straight ahead like them. I thought maybe that way I would get a chance to escape."

"*Smart* girl," Rashel said. "And the guy—was it Quinn?"

"No. I never saw Quinn again. It was this blond guy named Ivan from the club; I called him Ivan the Terrible. And there was a girl who brought us food sometimes—I don't know her name, but I used to see her at the club, too. They were like Quinn; they each had their own little group, you know."

At least two others besides Quinn, Rashel thought. Probably more.

"They didn't hurt us or anything, and the office was heated, and the food was okay—but I was so *scared*," Daphne said. "I didn't understand what was going on at all. I didn't know where Quinn was, or how I'd gotten there, or what they were going to do with us." She swallowed.

Rashel didn't understand that last either. What *were* the vampires doing with the girls in the warehouse? Obviously not killing them out of hand.

"And then last night . . ." Daphne's voice wobbled and she stopped to breathe. "Last night Ivan brought this new girl in. He carried her in and put her on a cot. And . . . and . . . then he bit her. He bit her on the neck. But it wasn't a game." The cornflower-blue eyes stared into the distance, wide with remembered horror. "He *really* bit her. And blood came out and he drank it. And when he lifted his head up I saw his teeth." She started to hyperventilate.

"It's okay. You're safe now," Rashel said.

"I didn't *know*! I didn't know those things were real! I thought it was all just . . ." Daphne shook her head. "I didn't know," she said softly.

"Okay. I know it's a big shock. But you've been dealing with it really well. You managed to get away from the truck, didn't you? Tell me about the truck."

"Well—that was tonight. I could tell day from night by looking at this little window high up. Ivan and the girl came and took the chains off us and made us all get in the truck. And then I was *really* scared—I didn't know where they were taking us, but I heard something about a boat. And I knew wherever it was, *I didn't want to go*."

"I think you're right about that."

Daphne took another breath. "So I watched the way Ivan shut the door of the truck. He was in back with us. And when he was looking the other way, I sort of jumped at the door and got it open. And then I just fell out. And then I ran—I didn't know which way to go, but I knew I had to get away from them. And then I saw you. And . . . I guess you saved my life." She considered. "Uh, I don't know if I remembered to say thank you."

Rashel made a gesture of dismissal. "No problem. You saved yourself, really." She frowned, staring at a drop of chocolate on the plastic table without seeing it.

"Well. I *am* grateful. Whatever they were going to do to me, I think it must have been pretty awful." A pause, then she said, "Uh, Rashel? Do *you* know what they were going to do to me?"

"Hm? Oh." Rashel nodded slowly, looking up from the table. "Yes, I think so."

CHAPTER 8

"ell?" Daphne said.

"I think it's the slave trade."

And, Rashel thought, I think I was right—this is something big.

The Night World slave trade had been banned a long time ago—back in medieval days, if she remembered the stories correctly. The Council apparently had decided that kidnapping humans and selling them to Night People for food or amusement was just too dangerous. But it sounded as if Quinn might be reviving it, probably without the Council's permission. How very enterprising of him.

I was right about killing him, too, Rashel thought. There's no choice now. He's as bad as I imagined—and worse.

Daphne was goggling. "They were going to make me a *slave*?" she almost yelled.

"Shh." Rashel glanced at the man behind the doughnut

counter. "I think so. Well—a slave and a sort of perpetual food supply if you were sold to vampires. Probably just dinner if you were going to werewolves."

Daphne's lips repeated *werewolves* silently. But Rashel was speaking again before she could ask about it.

"Look, Daphne—did you get *any* idea about where you might be going? You said they mentioned a boat. But a boat to where? What city?"

"I don't *know.* They never talked about any city. They just said the boat was ready . . . and something about an *aunt-clave.*" She pronounced it *ont-clave.* "The girl said, 'When we get to the *aunt-clave* . . .'" Daphne broke off as Rashel grabbed her wrist.

"An enclave," Rashel whispered. Thin chills of excitement were running through her. "They were talking about an enclave."

Daphne nodded, looking alarmed. "I guess."

This was big. This was . . . bigger than big. It was incredible.

A vampire enclave. The kidnapped girls were being taken to one of the hidden enclaves, one of the secret strongholds no vampire hunter had ever managed to penetrate. No human had even discovered the location of one.

If I could get there . . . if I could get in . . .

She could learn enough to destroy a whole town of vampires. Wipe an enclave off the face of the earth. She *knew* she could.

"Uh, Rashel? You're hurting me."

"Sorry." Rashel let go of Daphne's arm. "Now, listen," she said fiercely. "I saved your life, right? I mean, they were going to do terrible things to you. So you owe me, right?"

"Yeah, sure; sure, I owe you." Daphne made pacifying motions with her hands. "Are you okay?"

"Yes. I'm fine. But I need your help. I want you to tell me everything about that club. *Everything* I need to get in—and get chosen."

Daphne stared at her. "I'm sorry; you're crazy."

"No, no. I know what I'm doing. As long as they don't know I'm a vampire hunter, it'll be okay. I *have* to get to that enclave."

Daphne slowly shook her blond head. "What, you're going to, like, slay them all? By yourself? Can't we just tell the *police*?"

"Not all by myself. I could take a couple of other vampire hunters to help me. And as for the police . . ." Rashel stopped and sighed. "Okay. I guess there are some things I should explain. Then maybe you'll understand better." She raised her eyes and looked at Daphne steadily. "First, I should tell you about the Night World. Look, even before you met those vampires, didn't you ever have the feeling that there was something *eerie* going on, right alongside our world and all mixed up in it?"

She made it as simple as she could, and tried to answer

Daphne's questions patiently. And at last, Daphne sat back, looking sick and more frightened than Rashel had seen her yet.

"They're *all over*," Daphne said, as if she still didn't believe it. "In the police departments. In the government. And nobody's ever been able to do anything about them."

"The only people who've had any success are the ones who work secretly, in small groups or alone. We stay hidden. We're very careful. And we weed them out, one by one. That's what it means to be a vampire hunter."

She leaned forward. "Now do you see why it's so important for me to get to that enclave? It's a chance to get at a whole bunch of them all at once, to wipe out one of their hiding places. Not to mention stopping the slave trade. Don't you think it should be stopped?"

Daphne opened her mouth, shut it again. "Okay," she said finally, and sighed. "I'll help. I can tell you what to talk about, how to act. At least what worked for me." She cocked her head. "You're going to have to dress differently. . . ."

"I'll get a couple of other vampire hunters and we'll meet tomorrow after school. Let's say six-thirty. Right now, I'm taking you home. You need to sleep." She waited to see if Daphne would object, but the other girl just nodded and sighed again.

"Yeah. You know, after some of the things I've learned, home's starting to look good."

"Just one more thing," Rashel said. "You can't tell anybody

about what happened to you. Tell them anything—that you ran away, whatever—but not the truth. Okay?"

"Okay."

"And especially don't tell anyone about me. Got it? My life may depend on it."

"Elliot's not here." The voice on the telephone was cold and as hostile as Rashel had ever heard it.

"Vicky, I need to talk to him. Or *somebody*. I'm telling you, this is our chance to get to an enclave. The girl from the warehouse *heard* them talking about it." It was Friday afternoon and Rashel was phoning from a booth near her school.

Vicky was speaking heavily. "We staked out that street for days and didn't see anything, but *you* just happened to be in the right place at the right time to help a girl escape."

"Yes. I already told you."

"Well, that was convenient, wasn't it?"

Rashel gripped the handset more tightly. "What do you mean?"

"Just that it would be a very dangerous thing, going to a vampire enclave. And that a person would have to really *trust* whoever was giving them the information about it. You'd have to be sure it wasn't a trap."

Rashel stared at the phone buttons, controlling her breathing. "I see."

"Yes, well, you don't have much credibility around here

anymore. Not since letting that vampire get away. And this sounds like just the sort of thing you'd do if you *were* in on it with them."

Great, Rashel thought. I've managed to convince her that I really am a vampire sympathizer. Aloud she said, "Is that what Nyala is telling everybody? That I'm working with the Night World?"

"I don't know *what* Nyala is doing." Vicky sounded waspish and a little uneasy. "I haven't seen her since Tuesday and nobody answers at her house."

Rashel tried to make her voice calm and reasonable. "Will you at least tell Elliot what I'm doing? Then he can call me if he wants to."

"Don't hold your breath," Vicky said, and hung up.

Great. Terrific. Rashel replaced the handset wondering if she wasn't supposed to hold her breath until Elliot called, or until Vicky passed on the message.

One thing was clear: she couldn't count on any help from the Lancers. Or any other vampire hunters. Nyala could be spreading any kind of rumors, and Rashel didn't dare even call another group.

There was no choice. She'd have to do it alone.

That night she went to Daphne's house.

"Well, she's grounded," Mrs. Childs said at the door. She was a small woman with a baby in one hand, a Pampers in the other, and a toddler clutching her leg. "But I guess you can go upstairs."

Upstairs, Daphne had to chase a younger sister out of the bedroom before Rashel could sit down. "You see, I don't even have a *room* of my own," she said.

"And you're grounded. But you're alive," Rashel said, and raised her eyebrows. "Hi."

"Oh. Hi." Daphne looked embarrassed. Then she smiled, sitting cross-legged on her bed. "You're wearing normal clothes."

Rashel glanced down at her sweater and jeans. "Yeah, the ninja outfit's just my career uniform."

Daphne grinned. "Well, you're still going to have to look different if you're going to get into the club. Should we start now, or do you want to wait for the others?"

Rashel stared at a row of perfume bottles on the dresser across the room. "There aren't going to be any others."

"But I thought you said . . ."

"Look. It's hard to explain, but I've had a little problem with the vampire hunters around here. So I'm doing it without them. It's no problem. We can start now."

"Well . . ." Daphne pursed her lips. She looked different from the disheveled wild creature Rashel had rescued from the street last night. Her blond hair was soft and fluffy, her cornflower-blue eyes were large and innocent, her face was round and sweet. She was fashionably dressed and she seemed relaxed, in her own element in this normal teenager's room. It was Rashel who felt out of place.

"Well . . . do you want to just take along a friend or something?" Daphne asked.

"I don't have a friend," Rashel said flatly. "And I don't want one. Friends are people to worry about, they're *baggage*. I don't like baggage."

Daphne blinked slowly. "But at school . . ."

"I don't stay at schools more than one year at a time. I live with foster families, and I usually get myself sent to a new city every year. That way I stay ahead of the vampires. Look, this isn't about me, okay? What I want to know—"

"But . . ." Daphne was staring at the mirror. Rashel followed her gaze to see that the reflecting surface was almost completely covered by pictures. Pictures of Daphne with guys, Daphne with other girls. Daphne counted her friends in droves, apparently. "But doesn't that get *lonely*?"

"No, it doesn't get lonely," Rashel said through her teeth. She found herself getting rough with the lacy little throw pillow on her lap. "I like being on my own. Now are we done with the press conference?"

Looking hurt, Daphne nodded. "Okay. I talked with some people at school and everything at the club is going on the same as usual—except that Quinn hasn't been there since Sunday. Ivan and the girl were there Tuesday and Wednesday, but not Quinn."

"Oh, really?" That was interesting. Rashel had known from the beginning that her greatest problem was going to be Quinn. The other two vampires hadn't seen her—she didn't think they even realized that Daphne had run off with a vampire hunter last night. But Quinn had spoken to her. Had been . . . very close to her.

Still, what could he have seen in that cellar, even with his vampire vision? Not her face. Not even her hair. Her ninja outfit covered her from neck to wrist to ankle. All he could possibly know was that she was tall. If she changed her voice and kept her eyes down, he shouldn't be able to recognize her.

But it would be easier still if he weren't there in the first place, and Rashel could try her act on Ivan.

"That reminds me," she said. "Ivan and the girl—are their little groups into death, too?"

Daphne nodded. "Everybody in the whole place is, basically. It's that kind of place."

A perfect place for vampires, in other words. Rashel wondered briefly if the Night People owned the club or if some obliging humans had just constructed the ideal habitat for them. She'd have to check into that.

"Actually," Daphne was saying, a little shyly, "I've got a poem here for you. I thought you could say you wrote it. It would sort of prove you were into the same thing as the other girls."

Rashel took the piece of notebook paper and read:

"There's warmth in ice; there's cooling peace in fire,
And midnight light to show us all the way.
The dancing flame becomes a funeral pyre;
The Dark was more enticing than the Day."

She looked up at Daphne sharply. "You wrote this before you knew about the Night World?"

Daphne nodded. "It's the kind of thing Quinn liked. He used to say he was the darkness and the silence and things like that."

Rashel wished she had Quinn right there in the room, along with a large stake. These young girls were like moths to his flame, and he was taking advantage of their innocence. He wasn't even *pretending* to be harmless; instead he was encouraging them to love their own destruction. Making them think it was their idea.

"About your clothes," Daphne was going on. "My friend Marnie is about your size and she lent me this stuff. Try it on and we'll see if it looks right." She tossed Rashel a bundle.

Rashel unfolded it, examined it doubtfully. A few minutes later she was examining herself even more doubtfully in the mirror.

She was wearing a velvety black jumpsuit that clung to her like a second skin. It was cut in a very low V in front, but the sleeves reached down in Gothic points on the backs of her hands almost to the middle finger. Around her neck was a black leather choker that looked to her like a dog collar.

She said, "I don't know . . ."

"No, no, you look great. Sort of like a Betsey Johnson ultra model. Walk a little . . . turn around . . . okay, yeah. Now all we have to do is paint your fingernails black, add a little makeup, and—" Daphne stopped and frowned.

"What's wrong?"

"It's the way you walk. You walk like—well, like *them*, actually. Like the vampires. As if you're stalking something. And you don't ever make a noise. They're going to know you're a vampire hunter from the way you move."

It was a good point, but Rashel didn't know what to do about it. "Um . . ."

"I've got it," Daphne said brightly. "We'll put you in heels."

"*Oh*, no," Rashel said. "There is absolutely no way I'm going to wear those things."

"But it'll be perfect, see? You won't be *able* to walk normally."

"No, and I won't be able to run, either."

"But you aren't going there to run. You're going to talk and dance and stuff." Hands on her hips, she shook her head. "I don't know, Rashel, you really need somebody to go there with you, to help you with this stuff. . . ."

Daphne stopped and her eyes narrowed. She stared at the mirror for a moment, then she nodded. "Yeah. That's it.

There's no other choice," she said, expelling her breath. She turned to face Rashel squarely. "I'll just have to go with you myself."

"*What?*"

"You *need* somebody with you; you can't do this all alone. And there's nobody better than me. I'll go with you and this time we'll both get chosen."

Rashel sat on the bed. "I'm sorry; this time *you're* crazy. You're the last person the vampires would ever choose. You know all about them."

"But they don't know that," Daphne said serenely. "I told everybody at school today that I didn't remember anything that happened from Sunday on. I had to tell them something, you know. So I said that I never got to meet Quinn; that I didn't know what happened to me, but I woke up last night alone on this street in Mission Hill."

Rashel tried to think. Would any of the vampires believe this story?

The answer surprised her. They just might. If Daphne had begun to come out of the mind control while she was in the truck . . . if she had jumped out and started running, only to become fully conscious a little while later. . . . Yes. It could work. The vampires would assume that she'd have amnesia for the whole period she was in a trance, and maybe for a little before. It *could* work. . . .

"But it's too dangerous," she said. "Even if I let you go

to the club with me, I could never let you get chosen."

"Why not? You already said I must be resistant to their mind-control thingy, right?" Daphne's blue eyes were sparking with energy and her cheeks were flushed. "So that makes me perfect for the job. I can do it. I know I can help you."

Rashel stood helplessly. Take this fluffy bunny of a girl to a vampire enclave? Let her get sold as a slave to bloodsucking monsters? Ask her to fight ruthless snakes like Quinn?

"I like to work alone," she said in a hard voice.

Daphne folded her arms over her chest, refusing to be intimidated. "Well, maybe it's time you tried something different. Look, I've never met anyone like you. You're so independent, so adventurous, so—*amazing*. But even you can't do everything by yourself. I know I'm not a vampire hunter, but I'd like to be your friend. Maybe you should try trusting a friend this time."

Her eyes met Rashel's, and at that moment she didn't look like a fluffy bunny, but like a small, confident, and intelligent young woman.

"Besides, it was me who got kidnapped," Daphne said, shrugging. "Don't you think I should get to pay them back a little?"

Rashel caught herself almost grinning. She couldn't help liking this girl, or feeling a glow of warmth at her praise. But still . . . She drew in a careful breath and watched Daphne closely. "And you're not scared?"

"Of *course* I'm scared. I'd be stupid not to be. But I'm not so scared I can't go."

It was the right answer. Rashel looked around the cluttered lacy room and nodded slowly. At last she said, "Okay, you're in. Tomorrow's Saturday. We'll do it tomorrow night."

CHAPTER 9

How long since he'd identified with humans?

That had all stopped the day he stopped being human himself. Not at the *moment* he'd stopped being human, though. At first all his anger had been for Hunter Redfern. . . .

Waking up from the dead was an experience you don't forget. For Quinn, it happened in the Redfern cabin on a husk mattress in front of the fire.

He opened his eyes to see three beautiful girls leaning over him. Garnet, with her wine-colored hair shining in the ruby light, Lily with her black hair and her eyes like topaz, and Dove, his own Dove, brown-haired and gentle, with anxious love in her face.

That was when Hunter informed him that he'd been dead for three days.

"I told your father you'd gone to Plymouth; don't tell him otherwise. And don't try to move yet; you're too weak. We'll bring in something soon and you can feed." He stood behind his daughters, his arms around them, all of them looking down at Quinn. "Be happy. You're one of us now."

But all Quinn felt was horror—and pain. When he put his thumbs to his teeth, he found the source of the pain. His canine teeth were as long as a wildcat's and they throbbed at the slightest touch.

He was a monster. An unholy creature who needed blood to survive. Hunter Redfern had been telling the truth about his family, and he'd changed Quinn into one of them.

Insane with fury, Quinn jumped up and tried to get his hands around Hunter's throat.

And Hunter just laughed, fending off the attack easily. The next thing Quinn knew, he was running down the blazed trail in the forest, heading for his father's house. Staggering and stumbling down the trail, rather. He was almost too weak to walk.

Then suddenly Dove was beside him. Little Dove who looked as if she couldn't outrun a flower. She steadied him, held him up, and tried to convince him to go back.

But Quinn could only think of one thing: getting to his father. His father was a minister; his father would know what to do. His father would help.

And Dove, at last, agreed to go with him.

Later Quinn would realize that of course he should have known better.

They reached Quinn's home. At that point, if Quinn was afraid of anything, it was that his father wouldn't believe this wild story of bloodthirst and death. But one look at Quinn's new teeth convinced his father of everything.

He could recognize a devil when he saw one, he said.

And he knew his duty. Like every Puritan's, it was to cast out sin and evil wherever he found it.

With that, his father picked up a brand from the fire—a good piece of seasoned pine—and then grabbed Dove by the hair.

It was around this time that the screaming started, the screaming Quinn would be able to hear forever after if he listened. Dove was too gentle to put up much of a fight. And Quinn himself was too weak to save her.

He tried. He threw himself on top of Dove to shield her from the stake. He would always have the scar on his side to prove it. But the wood that nicked him pierced Dove to the heart. She died looking up at him, the light in her brown eyes going out.

Then everything was confusion, with his father chasing him, crying, brandishing the bloody stake pulled from Dove's body. It ended when Hunter Redfern appeared at the door with Lily and Garnet. They took Quinn and Dove home with them, while Quinn's father went running to the neighbors for help. He wanted help burning the Redfern cabin down.

That was when Hunter said it, the thing that severed Quinn's ties with his old world. He looked down at his dead daughter and said, "She was too gentle to live in a world full of humans. Do you think you can do any better?"

And Quinn, dazed and starving, so frightened and full of horror that he couldn't talk, decided then that he would. Humans were the enemy. No matter what he did, they would never accept him. He had become something they could only hate—so he might as well become it thoroughly.

"You see, you don't have a family anymore," Hunter mused. "Unless it's the Redferns."

Since then, Quinn had thought of himself only as a vampire.

He shook his head, feeling clearer than he had for days.

The girl had disturbed him. The girl in the cellar, the girl whose face he had never seen. For two days after that night, all he could think of was somehow finding her.

What had happened between them . . . well, he still didn't understand that. If she had been a witch, he'd have thought she bewitched him. But she was human. And she'd made him doubt everything he knew about humans.

She'd awakened feelings that had been sleeping since Dove died in his arms.

But now . . . now he thought it was just as well he hadn't been able to find her. Because the cellar girl wasn't just human, she was a vampire hunter. Like his father. His father, who, wild-eyed and sobbing, had driven the stake through Dove's heart.

As always, Quinn felt himself losing his grip on sanity as he remembered it.

What a pity that he'd have to kill the cellar girl the next time he saw her.

But there was no help for it. Vampire hunters were worse than the ordinary human vermin, who were just stupid. Vampire hunters were the sin and the evil that had to be cast out. The Night World was the only world.

And I haven't been to the club in a week, Quinn thought, showing his teeth. He laughed out loud, a strange and brittle sound. Well, I guess I'd better go tonight.

It's all part of the great dance, you see, he thought to the cellar girl, who of course couldn't hear him. The dance of life and death. The dance that's going on right this minute all over the world, in African savannas and Arctic snowfields and the bushes in Boston Common.

Killing and eating. Hunting and dying. A spider snags a bluebottle fly; a polar bear grabs a seal. A coyote springs on a rabbit. It's the way the world has always been.

Humans were part of it, too, except that they let slaughterhouses do the killing for them and received their prey in the form of McDonald's hamburgers.

There was an order to things. The dance required that someone be the hunter and someone else be the hunted. With all those young girls longing to offer themselves to the darkness, it would be *cruel* of Quinn not to provide a darkness to oblige them.

They were all only playing their parts.

Quinn headed for the club, laughing in a way that scared even him.

The club was only a few streets away from the warehouse, Rashel noted. Made sense. Everything about this operation had the stamp of efficiency, and she sensed Quinn's hand in that.

I wonder what he's getting paid to provide the girls for sale? she thought. She'd heard that Quinn liked money.

"Remember, once we get inside, you don't know me," she said to Daphne. "It's safer for both of us that way. They might suspect something if they knew that first you escaped and now you're turning up with a stranger."

"Got it." Daphne looked excited and a little scared. Under her coat, she was wearing a slinky black top and a brief skirt, and her black-stockinged legs twinkled as she ran toward the club door.

Under Rashel's coat, hidden in the lining, was a knife. Like her sword, it was made of lignum vitae, the hardest wood on earth. The sheath had several interesting secret compartments.

It was the knife of a ninja, and Sensei, who had taught Rashel the martial arts, wouldn't have approved at all. He wouldn't have approved of Rashel dressing like a ninja, either.

His own family had been samurai, and he'd taught her to fight with honor.

But then Sensei hadn't understood about vampires . . . until it was too late. They'd gotten him while he was asleep, after tracking Rashel back from a job.

Sometimes honor just won't cut it, Rashel thought as she walked toward the club, trying very hard not to fall off her high heels. Sometimes ya gotta fight dirty.

The entrance of the Crypt was a battered green door inset with a narrow cloudy window. The building looked as if it had once been a small factory—there was still an ancient wooden sign on the door that read NO ADMITTANCE, AUTHORIZED PERSONNEL ONLY.

Rashel's lip quirked as she knocked just below the sign.

The next instant she had the feeling that she was being inspected, evaluated. She stood with her hands in her coat pockets, the coat held open to show the velvet jumpsuit underneath. She tried to assume a Daphne-like expression.

Light played on the other side of the cloudy window: somber light, deep purples and blues with an occasional flash of sullen red. Rashel gritted her teeth and waited.

Finally the door opened.

"Hi, how're you doing, where'd you hear about us?" the blond boy on the other side of the door said, holding out a hand. He said it all in a mumble, as if by rote, and his body seemed cast in a permanent slouch. But there was something sharp in his eyes, and Rashel had to control her instinct to fall into a fighting stance.

He was a vampire.

No doubt about it. Those silvery-blue eyes belonged to a killer.

Ivan the Terrible, I presume, Rashel thought. She gave him her hand, making it limp and passive. Then she smiled at him.

"A friend of mine said that this place was seriously cool," she said in her new voice, which was supposed to be light and musical like Daphne's. Instead, she noticed regretfully, it sounded a bit like the light musical purr of a cat to its dinner.

"So I just had to come, and I really like what I see. In fact, I'd like to get to know *you* better." She stepped closer to Ivan and smiled again. Should she bat her eyelashes?

Ivan looked both interested and slightly alarmed. "Who's your friend?"

Gazing into his eyes, Rashel said, "Marnie Emmons." She knew Marnie wasn't there that night.

Ivan the Terrible nodded and gestured her in. "Have fun. And, uh, maybe I'll see you sometime later."

Rashel said, "Oh, I hope so," and swept in.

She had passed the first test. She had no doubt that if Ivan hadn't approved of her, she'd be outside on the pavement right now. And since Daphne had made it in, too, her story must have passed inspection. That was a relief.

Inside, the place looked like hell. Not a shambles. It literally looked like Hell. Hades. The Underworld. The lights turned it into a place of infernal fire and twisting purple shadows. The music was weird and dissonant and sounded to Rashel as if it were being played backward.

She caught scraps of conversation as she walked across the floor.

". . . going out Dumpster diving later . . ."

". . . no money. So I gotta jack somebody . . ."

". . . told Mummy I'd be at the key-club meeting . . ."

You get a real cross section here, she thought dryly.

Everybody had one thing in common, though; they were young. Kids. The oldest looked about eighteen. The youngest—well, there were a few girls Rashel would put at twelve. She had an impulse to go back and insert something wooden into Ivan.

A slow fire that had started in her chest when she first heard about the Crypt was burning hotter and hotter with everything she saw here. This entire place is a snare, a gigantic Venus flytrap, she thought as she took off her coat and added it to a pile on the floor.

But if she wanted to shut it down, she had to stay cool, stick to her plan. Standing by a cast-iron column, she scanned the room for vampires.

And there, standing with a little group that included Daphne, was Quinn.

It gave Rashel an odd shock to see him, and she wanted to look away. She couldn't. He was laughing, and somehow *that* caught hold of her like a fishhook. For a moment the morbid lighting of the room seemed rainbow-colored in the radiance shed by that laughter.

Appalled, Rashel realized that her face had flushed and her heart was beating fast.

I *hate* him, she thought, and this was true. She did hate him for what he was doing to her. He made her feel unmoored and adrift. Confused. Helpless.

She understood why those girls were clustered around him, longing to fling themselves into his darkness like a bunch of virgin sacrifices jumping into a volcano. I mean, what else do you *do* with a guy like that? she thought.

Kill him. It would be the only solution even if he weren't a vampire, she decided with sudden insane cheer. Because prolonged contact with that smile was obviously going to *annihilate* her.

Rashel blinked rapidly, getting a grip on herself. All right. Concentrate on that, on the job to be done. She was going to have to kill him, but not now; right now she had to get herself chosen.

Walking carefully on her heels, she went over to join Quinn's group.

He didn't see her at first. He was facing Daphne and a couple of other girls, laughing frequently—too frequently. He looked wild and a little feverish to Rashel. A sort of devilish Mad Hatter at an insane tea party.

". . . and I just felt so totally awful that I didn't get to meet you," Daphne was saying, "and I just wish I knew what *happened*, because it was just so seriously weird . . ."

She was telling her story, Rashel realized. At least none of the people listening seemed openly suspicious.

"I haven't seen you here before," came a voice behind her.

It belonged to a striking girl with dark hair, very pale skin, and eyes like amber or topaz . . . or a hawk's. Rashel froze, every muscle tensing, trying to keep her face expressionless.

Another vampire.

She was sure of it. The camellia-petal skin, the light in the eyes . . . this must be the girl vampire who'd brought Daphne food in the warehouse.

"No, this is my first time," Rashel said, making her voice light and eager. "My name's Shelly." It was close enough to her own name that she would turn automatically if anyone said it.

"I'm Lily." The girl said it without warmth, and those hawklike eyes continued to bore straight into Rashel's.

Rashel had to struggle to stay on her feet.

It's *Lily Redfern,* she thought, working desperately to keep an idiot smile plastered on her face. I know it is. How many Lilys can there be who'd be working with Quinn?

I've got a Redfern right here in front of me. I've got Hunter Redfern's *daughter* here.

For an instant she was tempted to simply make a dash for her knife. Killing a celebrity like Lily seemed almost worth giving up the enclave.

But on the other hand, Hunter Redfern was a moderate sort of vampire, with a lot of influence on the Night World Council. He helped keep other vampires in line. Striking at him through his daughter would just make him mad, and then he might start listening to the Councilors who wanted to slaughter humans in droves.

And Rashel would lose any hope of getting at the heart of the slave trade, where the real scum were.

I hate politics, Rashel thought. But she was already beaming at Lily, prattling for all she was worth. "It was my friend Marnie who told me about this place, and I'm really glad I came because it's even better than I thought, and I've got this poem I wrote—"

"Really. Well, I'm dying *not* to hear it," Lily said. Her hawklike eyes had lost interest. Her face was filled with open contempt—she'd dismissed Rashel as a hopeless fawning idiot. She walked away without glancing back.

Two tests passed. One to go.

"That's what I like about Lily. She's just so absolutely cold," a girl beside Rashel said. She had wavy bronze hair and bee-stung lips. "Hi, I'm Juanita," she added.

And she's serious, Rashel thought as she introduced herself. Quinn's group had noticed her at last, and they all seemed to agree with Juanita. They were fascinated by Lily's cold personality, her lack of feeling. They saw it as strength.

Yeah, because feeling hurts. Maybe I should worship her, too, Rashel thought. She was finding too many things in common with these girls.

"Lily the Ice Princess," another girl murmured. "It's like she's not even really from earth at all. It's like she's from another planet."

"Hold that thought," a new voice said, a crisp, laughing, slightly insane voice. The effect it had on Rashel was remarkable. It made her back stiffen and sent tingles up her palms. It closed her throat.

Okay, test number three, she thought, drawing on every ounce of discipline she'd learned in the martial arts. Don't lose *zanshin*. Stay loose, stay frosty, and go with it. You can do this.

She turned to meet Quinn's eyes.

CHAPTER 10

O r not to meet them so much as graze past them, before concentrating on his chin. She didn't dare stare directly into them for long.

"Maybe she *is* from another planet," Quinn was saying to the girl. "Maybe she's not human. Maybe I'm not, either."

That's right, Rashel thought. Make fun of them by telling them a truth they won't believe.

But, she noticed, Quinn looked more as if he didn't care what they found out than as if he were mocking them. "Maybe she's from another *world*. Did you ever think of that?"

Rashel was confused again. Quinn seemed to be trying to get himself killed. He appeared to be verging on telling these girls about the Night World, and under the laws of the Night World, that was punishable by death.

You're really slipping, Rashel thought. First the slave

trade, now this. I thought you were supposed to be such a stickler for the law.

"There are darker dimensions," Quinn was confiding to the group, "than you have ever imagined. But, you see, it's all part of life's grand design, so *it's all right.* Did you know"—he put his arm around a girl's shoulders, gesturing outward as if inviting her to look at some horizon—"that there's a certain kind of wasp that lays its eggs in the body of a caterpillar? A live caterpillar. And it stays alive, you see, while the eggs hatch and the little waspettes eat it from the inside out. Now, who do you think invented that?"

Rashel wondered if vampires could get drunk.

"That would probably be the most horrible way to die," Daphne chimed in, her musical voice ghoulish. "Being eaten by insects. Or maybe being burned."

"It would probably depend on how fast you burned," Quinn said meditatively. "A flash of fire—high enough temperature— you burn the nerves out in the first few seconds. Slow baking would be different."

"I'm writing a poem about fire," Rashel said. She was surprised to find that she was annoyed because Quinn didn't really seem to have noticed her. On second thought, she *should* be annoyed; her plan depended on him not only noticing but choosing her.

She was going to have to capture his attention.

"Do you have it with you?" Daphne was asking helpfully.

"No, but I can tell you the beginning," Rashel said. She braced herself to look at Quinn as she recited:

"There's warmth in ice; there's cooling peace in fire,
And midnight light to show us all the way.
The dancing flame becomes a funeral pyre;
The Dark was more enticing than the Day."

Quinn blinked. Then he smiled, and he looked Rashel over, clearly taking notice of the velvet jumpsuit and ending with her face. He looked everywhere . . . except into her eyes.

"That's right; you've got it," he said with that same brittle exhilaration. "And there's plenty of dark out there for *everyone*."

Rashel's worry that he might look too deep if he met her gaze was groundless. Quinn didn't seem to be really seeing anybody here.

"There *is* plenty of darkness," Rashel said. She moved toward him, feeling strangely brave. Her instincts sensed a weakness in him, a flaw. "It's everywhere. It's inescapable. So the only thing we can do is embrace it." She was standing right in front of him now, looking at his mouth. "If we hold it close, it won't hurt so much."

"Well. Exactly." Quinn showed his teeth, but it wasn't the manic smile. It was a grimace. He didn't look happy anymore; suddenly, for just an instant, he looked tired and sick. He was almost leaning away from Rashel.

"I came here so I could do that," Rashel said in a sultry voice. She was scaring herself a little. In the name of the charade, she was doing everything she could to seduce him—but it was surprisingly easy and surprisingly enjoyable. There was a sort of tingling all over her body, as if the jumpsuit had picked up a charge.

"I came to look for the darkness," she said. Softly.

Quinn laughed abruptly. The feverish good humor came flooding back. "And you found it," he said. He went on laughing and laughing, and he reached out to touch Rashel's cheek.

Don't let him touch you!

The thought flashed through Rashel's mind and communicated to her muscles in an instant. Without knowing how she knew, she was certain that if he touched her, it would all be over. It was skin-to-skin contact that had nearly fried every circuit in her brain before.

She danced back from his fingertips and smiled teasingly, while her heart tried to pound its way out of her chest.

"This place is so crowded," she said throatily.

"Huh? Oh. Then why don't we schedule something more private? I could pick you up tomorrow night. Say seven o'clock in the parking lot."

Bingo.

"But, Quinn." It was Daphne, looking aggrieved. "You told *me* to meet you tomorrow." She trembled her chin.

Quinn stared at her, and for once, Rashel could read

his face easily. He was thinking that anybody *that* stupid deserved it.

"Well, you can both come," he said expansively. "Why not? The more the merrier."

He walked away laughing and laughing.

Rashel watched him go, resisting an impulse to shake her head. She'd done it; she'd passed the last test and been chosen. So why was her heart still pounding?

She glanced out of the side of her eye at Daphne. "Well, I don't know about anybody else, but I've had enough excitement for tonight." She went to get her coat, with the rest of Quinn's coterie glaring jealously after her.

She had one enjoyable experience on the way out. Ivan, still slouching, tried to stop her at the door.

"Shelly, hey. I thought we were going to get to know each other better."

Rashel didn't need him anymore; she had her invitation. "I'd rather get to know a head louse," she said in her sweet chatty voice, and she stepped on his foot hard with her high heel.

In the car, she waited a full twenty minutes, watching the front of the club, before Daphne joined her.

"Sorry, but I didn't want anybody to think we were leaving together."

"You did a great job," Rashel said, driving away. "You even managed to get both of us invited to meet Quinn together— that was dangerous, but it worked. The only thing that surprised me is that he invited us in front of everybody. Is that how he did it before?"

"No. Not at all. Last time, he sort of whispered it to me when nobody was around. But, you know, nothing was normal tonight. I mean, he usually asks new girls questions—I guess to figure out if they have families who'll miss them. And he isn't usually that—that . . ."

"Manic?"

"Yeah. I wonder what's going on with him?"

Rashel pressed her lips together and stared straight ahead through the windshield.

"You sure you want to go through with this?"

It was Sunday night and they were nearing the parking lot of the Crypt.

"I've told you and told you," Daphne said, "I'm ready. I can do it."

"Okay. But, listen, if there's any trouble, I want you to run. Run away from the club and don't look back for me. All right?"

Daphne nodded. At Rashel's suggestion, she was wearing something more sensible tonight: black pants heavy enough to provide some warmth, a dark sweater, and shoes she could run in. Rashel was dressed the same way, except that she was wearing high boots. The knife was in one.

"You go first," Rashel said, parking a street away from the club. "I'll come in a minute."

She watched Daphne walk away, hoping she wasn't going to get this little blond bunny killed.

She herself was the danger. Quinn was going to use mind control on them to get them to go to the warehouse quietly. And Rashel wasn't sure what would happen when he did it.

Just don't let him touch you, she told herself. You can carry it off as long as he doesn't touch you.

Five minutes later, she started toward the Crypt.

Quinn was in the dark parking lot, standing by a silvery-gray Lexus. As Rashel reached the car, she saw the pale blob of Daphne's face through the window.

"I almost thought you weren't coming." There was now a sort of savagery mixed in with Quinn's lunatic good humor. As if he were angry she wasn't smart enough to save herself.

"Oh, I wouldn't miss this for the world." Rashel kept her eyes on the car. She wanted to get this over with. "Are we going somewhere?"

There was that tiny hesitation that seemed to come every time she spoke to him, as if it were taking him a minute to focus. Or as if he were trying to figure something out, she thought nervously.

Then he answered smoothly, "Oh, right, get in."

Rashel got in. She glanced once at Daphne in the backseat. Daphne said, "What's up?" in a chirpy voice laced with feminine rivalry.

Good girl.

Quinn was getting in the driver's side. Once the door was

shut, he turned the engine on to run the heater. The windows immediately began to fog.

Rashel sat in a state of continuing mind, ready for the unexpected at any moment.

Only the unexpected didn't come. Nothing came. Quinn was just sitting there in the driver's seat.

Watching her.

With a sudden void in her stomach that threatened her *zanshin*, Rashel realized that it was too dark. Too *familiar*. They were sitting here together in silence, so close, visible to each other only in silhouette, just as they had in the cellar. She could almost *feel* Quinn's confusion as he tried to figure out what was bothering him.

And Rashel was afraid to say anything, afraid that her chirpiest voice wouldn't be a good-enough disguise. The horrible feeling of connection was mounting, like some giant green wave looming over them both. In a moment it would break, and Quinn would say, "I know you," and switch on the light to see the face without the veil.

Rashel's fingers edged toward her knife.

Then, through the electric buzzing in her ears, she heard Daphne say, "You know, I just love this car. I bet it goes really fast, too. This is all so exciting—I'm just so glad I *got* here this time. Not like last week."

She went on, blathering easily, while Rashel sank back light-headed with relief. The connection was broken; Quinn was now looking at his instrument panel as if trying to escape the chatter. And now Daphne was talking about how exciting it was to ride in the dark.

Smart, smart girl.

Quinn had to interrupt her to say, "So, you two girls want to surrender to the darkness?" He said it as if he were asking if they wanted to order pizza.

"Yes," Rashel said.

"Oh, yes," Daphne said. "It's just like we always say. I think that would be just the most seriously cool—"

Quinn made a gesture at her as if to say, "For God's sake, shut up." Not a rough gesture. It was more like an exasperated choir director trying to get through to some soprano who wouldn't stop at the end of the measure. Stop *here*.

And Daphne shut up.

Like that.

As if he'd turned off a switch in her. Rashel twisted slightly to look at the backseat and saw that Daphne had slumped to one side, body limp, her breathing peaceful.

Oh, God, Rashel thought. She was used to the kind of mind control other vampires had tried on her. The persuasive, whispery-voice-in-the-head type. And when Quinn hadn't tried to use that, or to call for help in the cellar, she'd assumed he was low on telepathy.

Now she knew the truth. He packed a telepathic punch like a pile driver. No, like a karate blow: swift, precise, and deadly.

He turned to look at her, a dark shape against a lighter darkness. Rashel tried to brace herself.

"And the rest is silence," Quinn said, and gestured at her.

Rashel fell into a void.

She woke up as she was being carried into the warehouse. She had enough presence of mind not to open her eyes or make any other sign that she was conscious. It was Quinn carrying her; she could tell even with her eyes shut.

When he dumped her on a mattress, she deliberately fell so that her head was turned away from him and her hair was over her face.

She had a moment's fear that he was going to discover the knife in her boot when he shackled her ankles. But he didn't even roll up her pant leg. He seemed to be doing everything as quickly as possible, without really paying attention.

Rashel heard the shackle snap shut. She kept perfectly still.

She lay and listened as he brought Daphne in and chained her. Then she heard voices close by and the sound of other footsteps.

"Put that one down here—what happened to her purse?" That was Lily.

"It's still in the car." Ivan.

"Okay, bring it in with the other one. I'll do her feet."

Thump of a body hitting a mattress. Footsteps going away. The metallic clink of chains. Then a sigh from Lily. Rashel could imagine her straightening up and looking around in satisfaction.

"Well, that's it. Ivan's got number twenty-four in the car. I guess we're going to have one very happy client."

"Joy," Quinn said flatly.

Twenty-four? One client?

"I'll leave a message that everything's going to be ready for the big day."

"Do that."

"You're awfully moody, you know. It's not just me who's noticed it."

A pause, and Rashel imagined Quinn giving one of his black looks. "I was just thinking it was ironic. I turned down a job as a slave trader once. That was before. Do you remember before, Lily? When we lived in Charlestown and your sister Dove was still alive. A captain from Marblehead asked if I wanted to ship out to Guinea for some human cargo. Black gold, I think he called it. As I remember, I hit him on the nose. And Fight-the-Good-Fight-for-Faith Johnson reported me for brawling."

"Quinn, what's wrong with you?"

"Just reminiscing about the old days in the sunlight. Of course, you wouldn't know about that, would you? You're lamia; you were born this way. Technically, I suppose, you were born dead."

"And technically, *I* suppose, you're going peculiar: My father always said it would happen."

"Yes, and I wonder what your father would think about all this? His daughter selling humans for money. And to such a client, and for such a reason—"

At that moment, while Rashel was listening desperately, hanging on every word, heavy footsteps interrupted. Ivan had returned. Quinn broke off, and he and Lily remained silent as another body thumped on a bed.

Rashel cursed mentally. *What* client? *What* reason? She'd supposed the girls were being sold as regular house slaves or food supplies. But clearly that wasn't the case.

And then something happened that drove thoughts of the future right out of her mind. She heard footsteps next to her bed, and she was aware of someone leaning close. Not Quinn, the smell was wrong.

Ivan.

A rough hand grabbed her hair and pulled her head back. Another arm slid under her waist, lifting her up.

Panic shot through Rashel, and she tried to push it away. She forced herself to stay limp, eyes shut, arms dangling passively.

I ought to have been prepared for this.

She'd realized from the beginning that playing her part might include allowing herself to get bitten. To feel vampire teeth on her throat, to allow them to spill her blood.

But it had never happened to her before, and it took every ounce of her will to keep from fighting. She was scared. Her arched throat felt exposed and vulnerable, and she could feel a pulse beating in it wildly.

"What are you doing?"

Quinn's voice was sharp as the crack of glacier ice. Rashel felt Ivan go still.

"I've got something to settle with this girl. She's a smartass."

"Take your hands off her. Before I knock you through the wall."

"Quinn—" Lily said.

Quinn's voice was painfully distinct. "Drop her. Now."

Ivan dropped Rashel.

"He's right," Lily said coolly. "They're not for you, Ivan, and they have to be in perfect shape."

Ivan muttered something sullen and Rashel heard footsteps moving away. She lay and listened to her heart slowly calming.

"I'm going to get some sleep," Quinn said, sounding flat and dull.

"See you Tuesday," Lily said.

Tuesday, Rashel thought. Great. It's going to be a very long two days.

They were the most boring two days of her life. She got to know every corner of the small glass-windowed office. The windows were a problem, since she was never absolutely sure if Lily or Ivan were outside one of them, standing in the warehouse proper and looking through. She listened carefully for the warehouse doors, froze instantly at any suspicious sound, and trusted to luck.

Daphne woke up Monday morning. Rashel had her neck twisted sideways and was staring through the office glass up at the one tiny window set high in the warehouse wall. Just as it turned gray with dawn, Daphne sat up and screamed.

"Shh! It's all right! You're here in the warehouse with me."

"Rashel?"

"Yeah. We made it. And I'm glad you're awake."

"Are we alone?"

"More or less," Rashel said. "There are two other girls, but they're both hypnotized. You'll see when it gets lighter."

Daphne let out her breath. "Wow . . . we did it. That's great. So how come I'm so completely and utterly terrified?"

"Because you're a smart girl," Rashel said grimly. "Just wait until Tuesday when they take us out."

"Take us out where?"

"That's the question."

CHAPTER 11

The U-Haul whirred across smooth resonant pavement and Rashel tried to guess where they were. She had been drawing a map in her mind, trying to imagine each turn they made, each change of the road underneath them.

Ivan sat slouched, blocking the back doors of the truck. His eyes were small and mean, and they flickered over the girls constantly. In his right hand he held a taser, a handheld electrical stun gun, and Rashel knew he was dying to use it.

But the cargo was being very docile. Daphne was beside Rashel, leaning against her very slightly for comfort, her dark blue eyes fixed vacantly on the far wall. They were shackled together: although both Lily and Ivan had been checking Daphne constantly for signs of waking up, they were clearly taking no chances.

On the opposite side of the truck were the two other girls. One was Juanita, her wavy bronze hair tangled from two days of lying on it, her bee-stung lips parted, her gaze empty. The second girl was a towhead, with flyaway hair and Bambi eyes staring blankly. Ivan called her Missy.

She was about twelve.

Rashel allowed herself to daydream about things to do to Ivan.

Then she focused. The van was stopping. Ivan jumped up, and a minute later he was opening the back doors. Then he and Lily were unshackling the girls and herding them out, telling them to hurry.

Rashel breathed deeply, grateful for the fresh open air. Salty air. Keeping her gaze aimless and glassy, she looked around. It was twilight and they were on a Charlestown dock.

"Keep moving," Ivan said, a hand on her shoulder.

Ahead, Rashel saw a sleek thirty-foot power cruiser bobbing gently in a slip. A figure with dark hair was on the deck, doing something with lines. Quinn.

He barely glanced up as Ivan and Lily hustled the girls onto the boat, and he didn't help steady Missy when she almost lost her balance jumping from the dock. His mood had changed again, Rashel realized. He seemed withdrawn, turned inward, brooding.

"Move!" Ivan shoved her, and for an instant, Quinn's attention shifted. He stared at Ivan with eyes like black death, endless and fathomless. He didn't say a word. Ivan's hand dropped from Rashel's back.

Lily led them down a short flight of steps to a cramped but neat little cabin and gestured them to an L-shaped couch behind a dinette table. "Here. Sit down. You two here. You two there."

Rashel slipped into her seat and stared vacantly across at the sink in the tiny galley.

"You all stay here," Lily said. "Don't move. Stay."

She would have made a great slave overseer, Rashel thought. Or dog trainer.

When Lily had disappeared up the stairs and the door above had banged shut, Rashel and Daphne simultaneously let out their breath.

"You doing okay?" Rashel whispered.

"Yeah. A little shaky. Where d'you think we're going?"

Rashel just shook her head. Nobody knew where the vampire enclaves were. An idea was beginning to form in her mind, though. There must be a reason they were traveling by boat—it would have been safer and easier to keep the prisoners in the U-Haul. Unless they were going to a place you couldn't get to by U-Haul.

An island. Why shouldn't some of the enclaves be on islands? There were hundreds of them off the eastern coast.

It was a very unsettling thought.

On an island they would be completely isolated. Nowhere to escape to if things got bad. No possible hope of help from outside.

Rashel was beginning to regret that she'd brought Daphne into this. And she had the ominous feeling that when they got to their destination, she was going to regret it even more.

The boat sliced cleanly through the water, heading into darkness. Behind Quinn was the skyline of Boston, the city lights showing where the ocean ended and the land began. But ahead there was no horizon, no difference between sky and sea. There was only formless, endless void.

The inky blackness was dotted with an occasional solitary winking light—herring boats. They only seemed to make the vastness of empty water more lonely.

Quinn ignored Lily and Ivan. He was not in a good mood.

He let the cold air soak into him, permeating his body, mixing with the cold he felt inside. He imagined himself freezing solid—a rather pleasant thought.

Just get to the enclave, he thought emptily. Get it over with.

This last batch of girls had upset him. He didn't know why, and he didn't want to think about it. They were vermin. All of them. Even the dark-haired one who was so lovely that it was almost too bad she was certifiably insane. The little blond one was crazy, too. The one who, having had the luck to fall out of the frying pan once, had come right back, coated herself with butter and breadcrumbs, and jumped in again.

Idiot. Someone like that deserved . . .

Quinn's thought broke off. Somewhere deep inside him was a little voice saying that no one, however idiotic, deserved what was going to happen to those girls.

You're the idiot. Just get them to the enclave and then you can forget all this.

The enclave . . . it was Hunter Redfern who had first thought of enclaves on islands. Because of Dove, he'd said.

"We need a place where the Redferns can live safely, without looking over their shoulders for humans with stakes. An island would do."

Quinn hadn't objected to the classification of himself as a Redfern—although he had no intention of marrying Garnet or Lily. Instead he said, practically, "Fishermen visit those islands all the time. Humans are settling them. We'd have company soon."

"There are spells to guard places humans shouldn't go. I know a witch who'll do it, to protect Lily and Garnet."

"Why?"

Hunter had grinned. "Because she's their mother."

And Quinn had said nothing. Later he'd met Maeve Harman, the witch who had mingled her blood with the lamia. She didn't seem to like Hunter much, and she kept their youngest daughter, Roseclear, who was being raised as a witch, away from him. But she did the spell.

And they'd all moved to the island, where Garnet finally gave up on Quinn and married a boy from a nice lamia family.

Her children were allowed to carry on the Redfern name. And as time went on, other enclaves had sprung up. . . .

But none quite like the one Quinn was heading for now.

He shifted on his seat in the cockpit. Ahead, there was a horizon again. A luminous silver moon was rising above the pond-still dark water. It shone like an enchantment, as if to guide Quinn's way.

Scrrrunch.

Rashel winced as the boat docked. Somebody wasn't being careful. But they'd arrived, and it could only be an island. They'd been heading east for over two hours.

Daphne lifted her head weakly. "I don't care if they eat us the minute we get off, as long as I get to feel solid ground again."

"This practically is solid ground," Rashel whispered. "It's been dead calm the whole way."

"Tell that to my stomach." Daphne moaned, and Rashel poked her. Someone was coming down the stairs.

It was Lily. Ivan waited above with the taser. They herded the girls off the boat and up onto a little dock.

Rashel did her vacant-eyed staring around again, blessing the moonlight that allowed her to see.

It wasn't much of a dock. One wharf with a gas pump and a shack. There were three other powerboats in slips.

And that was all. Rashel couldn't see any sign of life. The

boats rode like ghost ships on the water. There was silence except for the slap of the waves.

Private island, Rashel thought.

Something about the place made the hair on the back of her neck rise.

With Lily in front and Ivan in back, the group was herded to a hiking trail that wound up a cliff.

It's just an island, Rashel told herself. You should be dancing with joy. This is the enclave you wanted to get to. There's nothing . . . *uncanny* . . . about this place.

And then, as they reached the top of the cliff, she saw the rocks. *Big* rocks. Monoliths that reminded her eerily of Stonehenge. It looked as if a giant had scattered them around.

And there were houses built among them, perched on the lonely cliff, looking down on the vast dark sea. They all seemed deserted, and somehow they reminded Rashel of gargoyles, hunched and waiting.

Lily was headed for the very last house on the sandy unpaved road.

It was one of those huge "summer cottages" that was really a mansion. A massive white frame house, two and a half stories high, with elaborate ornamentation.

Shock coursed through Rashel.

A frame house. *Wood.*

This place wasn't built by vampires.

The lamia built out of brick or fieldstone, not out of the

wood that was lethal to them. They must have bought this island from humans.

Rashel was tingling from head to toe. *This is definitely not a normal enclave. Where are all the people? Where's the town? What are we* doing *here?*

"Move, move." Lily marched them around the back of the house and inside. And at last, Rashel heard the sounds of other life. Voices from somewhere inside the house.

But she didn't get to see who the voices belonged to. Lily was taking them into a big old-fashioned kitchen, past a pantry with empty shelves.

At the end of the pantry was a heavy wooden door, and on a stool by the door was a boy about Rashel's age. He had bushy brown hair and was wearing cowboy boots. He was reading a comic book.

"Hey, Rudi," Lily said crisply. "How're our guests?"

"Quiet as little lambs." Rudi's voice was laconic, but he stood up respectfully as Lily went by. His eyes flickered over Rashel and the other girls.

Werewolf.

Rashel's instincts were screaming it. And the name . . . werewolves often had names like Lovell or Felan that meant wolf in their native language.

Rudi meant "famous wolf" in Hungarian.

Best guards in the world, Rashel thought grimly. *Going to be hard to get past him.*

Rudi was opening the door. With Lily prodding her from behind, Rashel walked down a narrow, extremely steep staircase. At the base of the stairway was another heavy door. Rudi unlocked it and led the way.

Rashel stepped into the cellar.

What she saw was something she'd never seen before. A large low-ceilinged room. Dimly lit. With two rows of twelve iron beds along opposite walls.

There was a girl in each bed.

Teenage girls. All ages, all sizes, but every one beautiful in her own unique way.

It looked like a hospital ward or a prison. As Rashel walked between the rows, she had to fight to keep her face blank. These girls were chained to the beds, and awake . . . and scared.

Frightened eyes looked at Rashel from every cot, then darted toward the werewolf. Rudi grinned at them, waving and nodding to either side. The girls shrank away.

Only a few seemed brave enough to say anything.

"Please . . ."

"How long do we have to stay here?"

"I want to go home!"

The last two beds in each row were empty. Rashel was put into one. Daphne looked both sick and frightened as the shackles closed over her ankles, but she went on gamely staring straight ahead.

"Sleep tight, girlies," Rudi said. "Tomorrow's a big day."

And then he and Lily and Ivan walked out. The heavy wooden door slammed behind them, echoing in the stone-walled cellar.

Rashel sat up in one motion.

Daphne twisted her head. "Is it safe to talk?" she whispered.

"I think so," Rashel said in a normal voice. She was staring with narrowed eyes down the rows of beds. Some of the girls were looking at them, some were crying. Some had their eyes shut.

Daphne burst out with the force of a breaking dam, *"What are they going to do to us?"*

"I don't know," Rashel said. Her voice was hard and flat, her movements disciplined and precise, as she slid the knife out of her boot. "But I'm going to find out."

"What, you're gonna saw through the chains?"

"No." From a guard on the side of the sheath, Rashel pulled a thin strip of metal. She bared her teeth slightly in a smile. "I'm going to pick the lock."

"Oh. Okay. Great. But then what? I mean, what's happening here? What kind of place is this? I was expecting some kind of—of Roman slave auction or something, with, like, everybody dressed in togas and vampires waving and bidding—"

"You may still see something like that," Rashel said. "I agree, it's weird. This is not a normal enclave. I don't know, maybe it's some kind of holding center, and they're going to take us someplace else to sell us. . . ."

"Actually, I'm afraid not," a quiet voice to her left said.

Rashel turned. The girl in the bed beside her was sitting up. She had flaming red hair, wistful eyes, and a diffident manner. "I'm Fayth," she said.

"Shelly," Rashel said briefly. She didn't trust anyone here yet. "That's Daphne. What do you mean, you're afraid not?"

"They're not taking us somewhere else to sell us." Fayth looked almost apologetic.

"Well, I'd like to know what they're going to do with us *here*," Rashel said. She sprung one lock on the shackles and jabbed the lockpick into the other. "Twenty-four girls on an island with one inhabited house? It's insane."

"It's a bloodfeast."

Rashel's hand on the lockpick went still.

She looked over at Fayth and said very softly, "What?"

"They're having a bloodfeast. On the spring equinox, I think. Starting tomorrow night at midnight."

Daphne was reaching across the gap for Rashel. "What, what? What's a bloodfeast? *Tell* me."

"It's . . ." Rashel dragged her attention from Fayth. "It's a feast for vampires. A big celebration, a banquet. Three courses, you know." She looked around the room. "Three girls. And there are twenty-four of us. . . ."

"Enough for eight vampires," Fayth said quietly, looking apologetic.

"So you're saying that they take a little blood from each

of three girls." Daphne was leaning anxiously toward Rashel. "That's what you're saying, right? Right? A little sip here, a little sip there—" She broke off as Rashel and Fayth both looked at her. "You're *not* saying that."

"Daphne, I'm sorry I got you into this." Rashel took a breath and opened the second lock on her shackles, avoiding Daphne's eyes. "The idea of a bloodfeast is that you drink the blood of three people in one day. All their blood. You drain them."

Daphne opened her mouth, shut it, then at last said pathetically, "And you don't burst?"

Rashel smiled bleakly in spite of herself. "It's supposed to be the ultimate high or something. You get the power of their blood, the power of their life force, all at once." She looked at Fayth. "But it's been illegal for a long time."

Fayth nodded. "So's slavery. I think somebody wants it to make a comeback."

"Any idea who?"

"All I know is that somebody very rich has invited seven of the most powerful made vampires here for the feast. Whoever he is, he really wants to show them a good time."

"To make an alliance," Rashel said slowly.

"Maybe."

"The made vampires ganging up against the lamia."

"Possibly."

"And the spring equinox . . . they're celebrating the anniversary of the first made vampire. The day Maya bit Thierry."

"Definitely."

"Just wait a minute," Daphne said. "Just everybody press pause, okay? How come you know about all this stuff?" She was staring at Fayth. "Made vampires, this vampires, that vampires, Maya . . . I never heard of any of these people."

"Maya was the first of the lamia," Rashel said rapidly, glancing back at her. "She's the ancestress of all the vampires who can grow up and have children—the *family* vampires. The made vampires are different. They're humans who get made into vampires by being bitten. They can't grow any older or have kids."

"And Thierry was the first human to get made into a vampire," Fayth said. "Maya bit him on the spring equinox . . . thousands of years ago."

Rashel was watching Fayth closely. "So now maybe you'll answer her question," she said. "How do you know all this? No humans know about Night World history—except vampire hunters and damned Daybreakers."

Fayth winced, and then Rashel understood why she seemed so apologetic. "I'm a damned Daybreaker."

"Oh, God."

"What's a Daybreaker?" Daphne prompted, poking Rashel.

"Circle Daybreak is a group of witches who're trying to get humans and Night People to . . . I don't know, all dance around and drink Coke together," Rashel said, nonplussed.

She was confused and revolted—this girl had seemed so normal, so sensible.

"To live in harmony, actually," Fayth said to Daphne. "To stop hating and killing each other."

Daphne wrinkled her nose. "You're a witch?"

"No. I'm human. But I have friends who're witches. I have friends who're vampires. I know lamia and humans who're soulmates—"

"Don't be disgusting!" Rashel almost shouted it. It took her a moment to get hold of herself. Then, breathing carefully, she said, "Look, just watch it, Daybreaker. I need your information, so I'm willing to work with you—temporarily. But watch the language or I'll leave you here when I get the rest of us out. Then you can live in harmony with eight vampires on your own."

Despite her effort at control, her voice was shaking. Somehow Fayth's words seemed to keep echoing in her mind, as if they had some strange and terrible importance. The word *soulmates* itself seemed to ricochet around inside her.

And Fayth was acting oddly, too. Instead of getting mad, she just looked at Rashel long and steadily. Then she said softly, "I see . . ."

Rashel didn't like the way she said it. She turned toward Daphne, who was saying eagerly, "So we're going to get out of here? Like a prison break?"

"Of course. And we'll have to do it *fast*." Rashel narrowed her eyes, trying to think. "I assumed we'd have more time . . . and there's that werewolf to get past. And then once we do get out, we're on an island. That's bad. We can't live long out in the wild—it's too cold and they'd track us. But there has to be a way. . . ." She glanced at Fayth. "I don't suppose there's any chance of other Daybreakers showing up to help."

Fayth shook her head. "They don't know I'm here. We'd heard that something was going on in a Boston club, that somebody was gathering girls for a bloodfeast. I came to check it out—and got nabbed before I made my first report."

"So we're on our own. That's all right." Rashel's mind was in gear now, humming with ideas. "Okay, first, we'll have to see what these girls can do—which of them can help us—"

Fayth and Daphne were listening intently, when Rashel was interrupted by the last thing she expected to hear in a place like this.

The sound of somebody shouting her name.

"Rashel! Rashel the Vampire Hunter! Rashel the Cat!"

CHAPTER 12

The voice was shrill, almost hysterical.

Unbalanced, Rashel thought dazedly, looking around. The sound of her secret being yelled out loud stunned her.

But just for an instant. The next moment she was moving swiftly between the rows of girls, looking for . . .

"Nyala!"

"I know why you're here!" Nyala sat up tensely. She looked just as she had when Rashel had seen her last, cocoa skin, queenly head, wide haunted eyes. She was even dressed in the same dark clothes she'd been wearing the night they caught Quinn.

"You're here because you were in on it all along! You pretend to be a vampire hunter—"

"Shut up!" Rashel said desperately. Nyala was shouting loud enough to be heard on the other side of the door. She knelt on Nyala's bed. "I'm not pretending, Nyala."

"Then how come you're free and we're all chained up? You're on their side! You call yourself the Cat—"

Rashel clamped a hand over her mouth.

"Listen to me," she hissed. Her heart was pounding. All the girls around her were staring and she expected to hear the cellar door open at any moment. "Nyala, *listen*. I know you don't like me or trust me—but you've got to stop yelling that. We may only have one chance to get out of here."

Nyala's chest was heaving. Her eyes, the color of dark plums, stared into Rashel's.

"I *am* a vampire hunter," Rashel whispered, willing Nyala to believe it. "I made a mistake letting that vampire go that night . . . I admit it. But I've been trying ever since to put things right. I got captured on purpose so I could find out what was going on here—and now I'm going to try to get all these girls free." She spoke slowly and distinctly, hoping Nyala could sense the truth of her words. "But, Nyala, if the Night People find out I'm a vampire hunter—much less the Cat— they are going to take me out and kill me right this minute. And then I don't think the rest of you have a chance."

She stopped to breathe. "I know it's hard to trust me. But please, please try. Do you think you can do that?"

A long pause. Nyala's eyes searched hers. Then, at last, Nyala nodded.

Rashel took her hand off Nyala's mouth. She sat back on the bed and they stared at each other.

"Thank you," Rashel said. "I'm going to need your help." Then she shook her head. "But how did *you* get here? How did you find the club?"

"I didn't find any club. I went back to that street with the warehouses on Wednesday. I thought maybe the vampire might come back. And then—somebody grabbed me from behind."

"Oh, Nyala." Wednesday night, Rashel thought. The night Daphne saw Ivan carry in a new girl and put her on a cot. That girl was Nyala. Rashel put a hand to her head. "Nyala—I almost saved you. I was there the next night—when Daphne fell out of the truck. Do you remember that? If I had only known . . ."

Nyala wasn't listening. "Then there was this whisper in my mind, telling me to sleep. And I couldn't move—I couldn't move my arms or my legs. But I wasn't asleep. And then he carried me into a warehouse and he bit me." Her voice was detached, almost pleasant. But her eyes froze Rashel in place.

"He bit me in the neck and I knew I was going to die, just like my sister. I could feel the blood coming out. I wanted to scream but I couldn't move. I couldn't do anything." She smiled oddly at Rashel. "I'll tell you a secret. It's still there, the bite. You can't see it, but it's still there." She turned her head to show a smooth unblemished neck.

"Oh, God, Nyala." Rashel had felt awkward trying to make gestures of comfort with Daphne, but now she didn't think. She just grabbed Nyala and hugged her hard.

"Listen to me," she said fiercely. "I know how you feel. I mean—no, I *don't* know, because it hasn't happened to me. But I'm *sorry.* And I know how you felt when you lost your sister." She leaned back and looked at Nyala, almost shaking her. "But we have to keep fighting. That's what's important right now. We can't let them win. Right?"

"Yes . . ." Nyala looked slowly around her bed, then up at Rashel. "Yes, that's right." Her eyes seemed to sharpen and focus.

"I'm making a plan to get out of here. And you have to stay calm and help me."

"Yes." Nyala sounded more definite this time. Then she smiled almost serenely and whispered, "And we'll get our revenge."

"Yeah." Rashel pressed her hand. "Somehow, we will. I promise you."

She walked back to her cot feeling eyes on her, although nobody asked any questions. Her own eyes were stinging.

What had happened to Nyala was her fault. The girl had already been on the edge, and because of Rashel, she'd gotten herself caught and attacked by a vampire. And now . . .

Now Rashel was worried about Nyala's sanity, even if they did manage to get off the island.

She's right about one thing, though, Rashel thought. Revenge. It's the only way to wipe out the things that have been done to these girls.

The fire in her chest was back—as if there were coals where her throat and heart ought to be. She let it harden her and burn away any stray thoughts of mercy for Quinn. Strange how she kept having thoughts of him, long after she'd made the resolution to kill him.

"Is she okay?" Daphne said worriedly. "I remember her from the warehouse."

"I know." Rashel took the lockpick and sat on Daphne's cot. She began to work at Daphne's shackles. "I don't know if she's okay. The vampires haven't been living in harmony with her." She glanced bitterly at Fayth, who just looked back gravely and steadily.

"Nobody thinks *all* the Night People are good," Fayth said. "Or all the humans. We don't approve of violence. We want to stop it all."

"Well, sometimes it takes violence to stop violence," Rashel said shortly. Fayth didn't answer.

"But why was she calling you a cat?" Daphne asked.

Rashel could feel Fayth's gaze on her. "*The* Cat. It's the name of a vampire hunter, one who's killed a lot of vampires."

Daphne's dark blue eyes widened slightly. "Is it you?"

Rashel sprung a lock. Somehow, with these two girls staring at her, she didn't feel quite so brash as she had a moment ago. She didn't feel terribly proud of being the Cat.

Without looking up, she said, "Yes." Then she glanced behind her at Fayth.

Fayth said nothing.

"There's going to be more killing before this is all done," Rashel said. "And I can't think of anybody who deserves it more than the vampires who brought us here. So you let me take care of that, and we won't argue about it. All right?" She sprung the other lock on Daphne's shackles. Daphne immediately stretched her legs luxuriously, then swung them to the floor. Fayth just nodded slowly.

"All right, then. Listen. The first thing we've got to do is get these girls organized." Rashel moved to work on Fayth's chains. "You're both good talkers. I want the two of you to go around and talk to them individually. I want to know who's going to be able to help us and who's still under mind control. I want to know who's going to be a problem. And I especially want to know who has any experience with boats."

"Boats?" Fayth said.

"No place on this island is safe. We have to get off. There are four boats in the harbor right now—if we can just find somebody to handle them." She looked from Daphne to Fayth. "I want you to bring me back at least two sensible girls who have some chance of not sinking a powerboat. Got it?"

Daphne and Fayth glanced at each other. They nodded. "Right, boss," Daphne murmured, and they started off.

Rashel sat, weighing a chain in her hand and thinking. There was no need to tell Daphne—yet—that she didn't plan to ship out with the boats.

• • •

Half an hour later Daphne and Fayth stood before her beaming. At least Daphne was beaming; Fayth was wearing that grave smile that was starting to drive Rashel crazy.

"Allow me to introduce Anne-lise," Daphne said, leading Rashel to a cot. "Originally a native of Denmark. She's done the race circuit in Antigua—whatever that means. Anyway, she says she can handle a boat."

The girl in the cot was one of the oldest there, eighteen or nineteen. She was blond, long-legged, and built like a Valkyrie. Rashel liked her at once.

"And this is Keiko over here," Fayth said in her simple way. "She's young, but she says she grew up around boats."

This one Rashel wasn't so sure about. She was tiny, with hair like black silk and a rosette mouth. She looked like a collector's doll. "How old are you?"

"Thirteen," Keiko said softly. "But I was born on Nantucket. My parents have a Ciera Sunbridge. I think I can do what you're asking—it's just the navigation that worries me."

"There isn't anybody else," Daphne stage-whispered in Rashel's ear. "So my advice is we trust the kid."

"I think the navigation will be straight west," Rashel said. She smiled reassuringly at Keiko. "Anyway, even the open ocean will be safer than here." She gestured to Daphne and Fayth to come back to their corner.

"Okay. Good job. You're right about trusting the kid; I

don't think we have any other choice. We definitely need two boats for all these girls. What else did you find out?"

"Well, the ones that are still under mind control are the ones that came with us," Daphne said. "Juanita and Missy. And the one that might cause trouble is your buddy Nyala. She's not completely hinged, if you know what I mean."

Rashel nodded. "The mind control may be a problem— how long did it take to wear off the others, Fayth?"

"A day or so after they came in. But that's not the only problem, Rashel. Anne-lise and Keiko think they can handle the boats—but not tonight. Not until tomorrow."

"We can't wait until tomorrow," Rashel said impatiently. "That's cutting it way too fine."

"I don't think we have a choice. Rashel, all these girls are tranquilized. Drugged."

Rashel blinked. "How—?" She shut her eyes. "Oh."

"The food," Fayth said, as Rashel nodded in resignation. "I realized right off that there was something in it. I think most of the girls know—and they'd *rather* be tranquilized than think about what's happening to them."

Rashel rubbed her forehead wearily. No wonder the girls hadn't asked her any questions. No wonder they weren't all screaming their heads off. They were doped to the gills.

"From now on we've got to keep them from eating," she said. "They need clear heads if we're going to escape." She looked at Fayth. "Okay. We wait. But that's going to make everything more dangerous. How often do they bring food in here?"

"Twice a day. Late morning and around eight at night. And then they take us to the bathroom two by two."

"Who does it?"

"Rudi. Sometimes he has another werewolf with him."

Daphne bit her lip anxiously. "Are we equipped for werewolves?"

Rashel smiled. Holding her knife, she pulled the decorative knob at the end of the sheath. It came off, revealing a metal blade. She reversed the knob and stuck it in the end of the sheath, so the blade stuck out like a bayonet. The hard wooden sheath itself was now a weapon.

"The blade is silver-coated steel," she said in satisfaction. "We are equipped for werewolves."

"You see?" Daphne said to Fayth. "This girl thinks of everything."

Rashel put the knife away. "All right. Let's talk to everybody again. I want to explain my plan. When we do this tomorrow night, it's going to take cooperation and precision."

And, she thought, a lot of luck.

"Chow time!"

Rudi walked between the rows of cots, tossing packages from a plastic bag to either side of him. He looked, Rashel thought, exactly like a trainer throwing herring to seals.

She scanned the aisle behind him. No other werewolf at the door. Good.

It had been a long night and a longer day. The girls were dizzy from lack of food, keyed up, and getting more tense with each untranquilized hour. A couple of them couldn't seem to shake their first impression of Rashel—which had come from Nyala's yelling.

"Eat up, girlies. Got to keep up your strength." A slightly warm foil package hit Rashel's lap, another hit the mattress. Same thing as brunch—hot dogs of the kind you get at a convenience store. Smeared with mustard and drugs. The girls had been surviving on the grapefruit juice he'd poured for them.

As Rudi turned to throw a package to Juanita, Rashel rose smoothly from her cot. In one motion she leaped and came down right on target.

"Don't make a sound," she said in Rudi's ear. "And don't even *think* about changing."

She had his arm twisted behind his back and the silver knife to his throat. Rudi didn't seem to know how he'd gotten there. There were hot dogs all over the floor.

"Now," Rashel said. "Let's talk about jujitsu. This is what you call a proper hold. Resistance to it will cause serious pain and quite possibly a fractured joint. Are you getting this, Rudi?" Rudi wiggled a little and Rashel exerted pressure upward on his knuckles. Rudi yelped and danced on his toes.

"Hush! What I want to know is, where is the other werewolf?"

"Guarding the dock."

"Who else is on the dock?"

"I—nobody."

"Is there anybody on the stairs or in the kitchen? Don't lie to me, Rudi, or I'll get annoyed."

"No. They're all in the gathering room."

Rashel nodded at Daphne. Daphne jumped out of her bed.

"Remember—quick and quiet everybody," she said, like a cheerleader who'd been promoted to drill sergeant.

Rashel felt Rudi boggle as every girl in the room kicked off her covers and stood up free.

"What the—what the—"

"Now, Rudi." Keeping his elbow trapped against her, Rashel exerted pressure again, moving him easily in the direction she wanted. "You go first. You're going to unlock the top door for us."

"Anne-lise and Keiko in front," Daphne said. "Missy right here. Let's go."

"I can't unlock it. I can't. They'll kill me," Rudi muttered, as Rashel moved him up the stairs.

"Rudi, look at these young women." Rashel swung him around so he had a good view of the prisoners behind him. They stood in one tense, clear-eyed, lightly breathing mass. "Rudi, if you don't unlock that door, I am going to tie you up and leave you alone with them . . . and this silver knife. I promise, whatever the vampires do to you won't be worse."

Rudi stared at the girls, who stared back at him. All ages, all sizes, united.

"I'll unlock the door."

"Good boy."

He fumbled getting the door open. When it was done, Rashel pushed him through first, looking tensely around. If there were vampires here, she had to change tactics fast.

The kitchen was empty—and music was blasting from somewhere inside the house. Rashel gave a quick savage grin. It was a lucky break she wouldn't have dared to pray for. The music might just save these girls' lives.

She pulled Rudi out of the way and nodded to Daphne.

Daphne stood at the head of the stairs, silently waving the girls out. Fayth led the way with the Valkyrie Anne-lise and the tiny Keiko behind her. The other girls hurried past, and Rashel was proud of how quiet they were.

"Now," she whispered, pushing Rudi back into the stairwell. "One last question. Who's throwing the bloodfeast?"

Rudi shook his head.

"Who hired you? Who bought the slaves? Who's the client, Rudi?"

"I don't know! I'm telling you! Nobody knows who hired us. It was all done on the phone!"

Rashel hesitated. She wanted to keep questioning him—

but right now the important thing was to get the girls off the island.

Daphne was still waiting in the kitchen, watching Rashel.

Rashel looked at her and then helplessly at Rudi's bushy brown head. She should kill him. It was the only smart thing to do, and it was what she'd planned to do. He was a conspirator in the plan to brutally murder twenty-four teenage girls—and he enjoyed it.

But Daphne was watching. And Fayth would give her that *look* if she heard Rashel had done him in.

Rashel let out her breath. "Sleep tight," she said, and hit Rudi on the head with the hilt of her knife.

He slumped unconscious and she shut the cellar door on him. She turned quickly to Daphne. "Let's go."

Daphne almost skipped ahead of her. They went out the back door and picked up the hiking path.

Rashel moved swiftly, loping across the beaten-down wild grass. She caught up to the string of girls.

"That's it, Missy," she whispered. "Nice and quiet. Nyala, you're limping; does your leg hurt? A little faster, everybody."

She made her way up to the front. "Okay, Anne-lise and Keiko. When we get there, I'll take care of the guard. Then you know what to do."

"Find which boats we can handle. Destroy whatever we can on the others and set them adrift. Then each take half the girls and head west," Anne-lise said.

"Right. If you can't make it to land, do your best and then call the Coast Guard."

"But not right away," Keiko put in. "Lots of islanders use ship-to-shore radio instead of telephones. The vampires may be monitoring it."

Rashel squeezed her shoulder. "Smart girl. I knew you were right for the job. And remember, if you *do* call the Coast Guard, don't give the right name of the boat and don't mention this island." It was perfectly possible that there were Night People in the Coast Guard.

They were almost at the bottom of the cliff, and so far no alarms had sounded. Rashel scanned the moving group again, then became aware that Daphne was behind her.

"Everything okay?"

"So far," Daphne said breathlessly. She added, "You're good at this, you know. Encouraging them and all."

Rashel shook her head. "I'm just trying to keep them together until they're not my problem anymore."

Daphne smiled. "I think that's what I just said."

The wharf was below them, the boats bobbing quietly. The ocean was calm and glassy. Silver moonlight gave the scene a postcard look. Ye Olde Quaint Marina, Rashel thought.

She loped to the front again. "Stay behind me, all of you." She added to Daphne, "I'll show you what I'm good at."

A few feet of rocks and sand and she was on the wharf.

Eyes on the shack, knife ready, she moved silently. She wanted to take care of the werewolf without noise, if possible.

Then a dark shape came hustling out of the shack into the moonlight. It took one look at Rashel and threw back its head to howl.

CHAPTER 13

Rashel knew she had to stop the guard before he could make a sound. The vampires' mansion was on the farther cliffs, overlooking open sea rather than the harbor, and the music ought to help drown outside noises—but the greatest danger was still that they would be heard before the girls could get away.

She launched herself at the werewolf, throwing a front snap kick to his chest. She could hear the air whoosh out as he fell backward. Good. No breath for howling. She landed with both knees on top of him.

"This is silver," she hissed, pressing the blade against his throat. "Don't make a noise or I'll use it."

He glared at her. He had shaggy hair and eyes that were already half-animal.

"Is there anybody on the boats?" When he didn't answer, she pressed the silver knife harder. *Is there?*"

He snarled a breathless "No." His teeth were turning, too, spiking and lengthening.

"Don't change—" Rashel began, but at that moment he decided to throw her off. He heaved once, violently.

A snap of her wrist would have plunged the silver blade into his throat even as she fell. Instead Rashel rolled backward in a somersault, tucking in her head and ending up on her right knee. Then, as the werewolf jumped at her, she slammed the sheathed knife upward against his jaw.

He fell back unconscious.

Too bad, I wanted to ask him about the client. Rashel looked shoreward, to see that Daphne, Anne-lise, and Nyala were on the pier with her. They were each holding a rock or a piece of wood broken from the jagged pilings of the wharf.

They were going to help me, Rashel thought. She felt oddly warmed by it.

"Okay," she said rapidly. "Anne-lise and Keiko, with me. Everybody else, stay. Daphne, keep watch."

In a matter of minutes she and the boating girls had checked the boats and found two with features they thought they could handle . . . and with fuel. Anne-lise had removed a couple of crucial engine pieces out of the others.

"Took out the impellers and the solenoids," she told Rashel mysteriously, holding out a grimy hand.

"Good. Let's set them adrift. Everybody else, get yourself on a boat. Find a place to sit fast and sit *down*." Rashel moved to the back of the group where Fayth had her arms around a couple of the girls who looked scared of setting out on the dark ocean. "Come on, people." She meant to herd them in front of her like chickens.

That was when it happened.

Rashel had an instant's warning—the faint crunch of sand on rock behind her. And then something hit her with incredible force in the middle of the back. It knocked her down and sent her knife flying.

Worse, it sent her mind reeling in shock. *She hadn't been prepared.* That instant's warning hadn't been enough—because she had already lost *zanshin.*

She no longer had the gift of continuing mind. She had lost her single purpose. In the old days she'd been fixed on one thing—to kill the Night People. There had been no hesitation, no confusion.

But now . . . she'd already faltered twice tonight, knocking the werewolves unconscious instead of killing them. She was confused, uncertain. And, as a result, unprepared.

And now I'm dead, she thought. Her numbed mind was desperately trying to recover and come up with a strategy.

But there was a wild snarling in her ear and a trail of hot pain down her back. Animal claws. There was a wolf on top of her.

Rudi had gotten loose.

Rashel gathered herself and bucked to throw the wolf off.

He slipped and she tried to roll out from under him, arms up to keep her throat protected.

The werewolf was too heavy—and too angry. He scrambled over her rolling body like a lumberjack on a log. His snarling muzzle kept darting for her throat in quick lunges. Rashel could see his bushy coat standing on end.

She felt fire across her ribs—his claws had torn through her shirt. She ignored it. Her one thought was to keep him away from her throat. Keeping an elbow up, she reached for the knife with her other hand.

No good. She hadn't rolled far enough. Her fingertips just missed the hilt.

And Rudi the wolf was right in her face. All she could see were sharp wet teeth, black gums, and blazing yellow eyes. Her face was misted with hot canine breath.

Every snap of those jaws made a hollow *glunk.* Rashel only had one option left—to block each lunge as it came. But she couldn't keep that up forever. She was already tiring.

It's over, she thought. The girls who might have helped her—Daphne and Nyala and Anne-lise—were at the far end of the wharf or on the boats. The other girls were undoubtedly too scared even to try. Rashel was alone, and she was going to die very soon.

My own stupid fault, she thought dimly. Her arms were shaking and bloodied. She was getting weaker fast. And the wolf knew.

Even as she thought it, she missed a block.

Her arm slipped sideways. Her throat was exposed. In slow motion she saw the jaws of the wolf opening wide, driving toward her. She saw the triumph in those yellow eyes. She knew, with a curious sense of resignation, that the next thing she would feel was teeth ripping through her flesh. The oldest way to die in the world.

I'm sorry, Daphne, she thought. I'm sorry, Nyala. Please go and be safe.

And then everything seemed to freeze.

The wolf stopped in midlunge, head jerking backward. Its eyes were wide and fixed. Its jaws were open but not moving. It looked as if it might howl.

But it didn't. It collapsed in a hot quivering heap on top of Rashel, legs stiff. Rashel scrambled out from under it automatically.

And saw her knife sticking out of the base of its skull.

Quinn was standing above it.

"Are you all right?"

He was breathing quickly, but he looked calm. Moonlight shone on his black hair.

The entire world was huge and quivering and oddly bright. Rashel still felt as if she were moving in slow motion.

She stared at Quinn, then looked toward the wharf.

Girls were scattered all over, as if frozen in the middle of running in different directions. Some were on the decks of the two remaining boats. Some were heading toward her. Daphne and Nyala were only fifteen feet away, but they were both staring at Quinn and seemed riveted in place. Nyala's expression was one of horror, hate—and recognition.

Waves hissed softly against the dock.

Think. Now *think*, girl, Rashel told herself. She was in a state of the strangest and most expanded consciousness she'd ever felt. Her hands were icy cold and she seemed to be floating—but her mind was clear.

Everything depended on how she handled the next few minutes.

"Why did you do that?" she asked Quinn softly. At the same time she shot Daphne the fastest and the most intense look of her life. It meant *Go now.* She willed Daphne to understand.

"You just lost a guard," she went on, getting up slowly.

Keep his eyes on you. Keep moving. Make him talk.

"Not a very good one," Quinn said, looking with fastidious disgust at the heap of fur.

Go, Daphne, *run,* Rashel thought. She knew the girls still had a chance. There were no other vampires coming down the path. That meant that Rudi had either been too angry to give a general alarm or too scared. That was one good thing about werewolves—they acted on impulse.

Quinn was the danger now.

"Why not a good one?" she asked. "Because he damaged the merchandise?" She lifted her torn shirt away from her ribs.

Quinn threw back his head and laughed. Something jerked in Rashel's chest, but she used the moment to change her position. She was right by the wolf now, with her left hand at the exact level of the knife.

"That's right," Quinn said. A wild and bitter smile still played around his lips. "He was presumptuous. You almost surrendered to the wrong darkness there, Shelly. By the way, where'd you get a silver knife?"

He doesn't know who I am, Rashel thought. She felt both relief and a strange underlying grief. He still thought she was some girl from the club—maybe a vampire hunter, but not *the* vampire hunter. The one he'd admitted was good.

So he's unprepared. He's off his guard.

If I can kill him with one stroke, before he calls to the other vampires, the girls may get away.

She glanced at the wharf again, deliberately, hoping to draw his gaze. But he didn't look behind him, and Daphne and the other stupid girls weren't leaving.

Refusing to go without her. Idiots!

Now or never, Rashel thought.

"Well, anyway," she said, "I think you saved my life. Thank you."

Keeping her eyes down, she held out her hand, her right hand. Quinn looked surprised, then reached out automatically.

With one smooth motion, like a snake uncoiling, Rashel attacked.

Her right hand drove past his hand and clamped on his wrist. Her left hand plunged down to grab the knife. Her fingers closed on the hilt and pulled—and the sheath with its attached silver blade stayed in the werewolf's neck.

Just as she'd planned. The knife itself came free, the real knife, the one made of wood.

And then Quinn tried to throw her and her body responded automatically. She was moving without conscious direction, anticipating his attacks and blocking them even as he started to make them. It transformed the fight into a dance. Faster than thought, graceful as a lioness, she countered every move he made.

Zanshin to the max.

She ended up straddling him with her knife at his throat.

Now. Fast. *End it.*

She didn't move.

You *have* to, she told herself. Quick, before he calls the others. Before he knocks you out telepathically. He can do it, you know that.

Then why isn't he trying?

Quinn lay still, with the point of the wooden knife in the hollow of his throat, just where his dark collar parted. His throat was pale in the moonlight and his hair was black against the sand.

Footsteps sounded behind Rashel. She heard rapid light breathing.

"Daphne, take the boats and go now. Leave me here. Do you understand?" Rashel spoke every word distinctly.

"But, Rashel—"

"Do it now!" Rashel put a force she hadn't known she had behind the words. She heard the quick intake of Daphne's breath, then footsteps scampering off.

All the while, she hadn't taken her eyes off Quinn.

Like everything else, the green-black blade of her knife was touched with moonlight. It seemed to shimmer almost liquidly. Lignum vitae, the Wood of Life. It would be death for him. One thrust would put it through his throat. The next would stop his heart.

"I'm sorry," Rashel whispered.

She was. She was truly sorry that this had to be done. But there was no way out. It was for Nyala, for all the girls he'd kidnapped and hunted and lured. It was to keep girls like them safe for the future.

"You're a hunter," Rashel said softly, trying for steadiness. "So am I. We both understand. This is the way it goes. It's kill or be killed. It all comes down to that in the end." She paused to breathe. *"Do* you understand?"

"Yes."

"If I don't stop you, you'll be a danger forever. And I can't let that happen. I can't let you hurt anyone else." She was aware that she was shaking her head slightly in her attempt to explain to him. Her lungs ached and there were tears in her eyes. "I *can't.*"

Quinn didn't speak. His eyes were black and bottomless. His hair was slightly mussed on his forehead, but he didn't show any other sign of just having been in a fight.

He's not going to struggle, Rashel realized.

Then make it quick and merciful. No need for him to feel the pain of wood through his throat. She switched her grip on the knife, raising it over his chest. Holding it with both hands, poised above his heart. One swift downward stroke and it would be over.

For the first time since she had killed a Night Person, she didn't say what she always said. She wasn't the Cat right now; this wasn't revenge for her. It was necessity.

"I'm sorry," she whispered, and shut her eyes.

He whispered, "This kitten has claws."

Rashel's muscles locked.

Her eyes opened.

"Go on," Quinn said. "Do it. You should have done it the first time." His gaze was as steady as Fayth's. She could see moonlight in his eyes.

He didn't look wild, or bitter, or mocking. He only looked serious and a little tired.

"I should have realized it before—that you were the one in the cellar. I knew there was something about you. I just couldn't figure out what. At least now I've seen your face."

Rashel's arms wouldn't come down.

What was wrong with her? Her resolve was draining away.

Her whole body was weak. She felt herself begin to tremble, and realized to her horror she couldn't stop it.

"Everything you said was true," he said. "This is how it has to end."

"Yes." Something had swollen in Rashel's throat and it hurt.

"The only other possibility is that I kill you. Better this way than that." He looked exhausted suddenly—or sick. He turned his head and shut his eyes.

"Yes," Rashel said numbly. He believed that?

"Besides, now that I *have* seen your face, I can't stand the sight of myself in your eyes. I know what you think of me."

Rashel's arms dropped.

But limply. The blade pointed upward, between her own wrists. She sat there with her knuckles on his chest and stared at a scraggly wild raspberry bush growing out of the cliff.

She had failed Nyala, and Nyala's sister, and countless other people. Other humans. When it really counted, she was letting them all down.

"I can't kill you," she whispered. "God help me, I can't."

He shook his head once, eyes still shut. She was open to attack, but he didn't do anything.

Then he looked at her. "I told you before. You're an idiot."

Rashel hit him under the jaw the way she'd hit the guard. The hilt of her dagger caught him squarely. He didn't move to avoid the blow.

It knocked him out cold.

Rashel wiped her cheeks and got up, looking around for something to tie him with. Her whole life was torn to pieces, falling around her. She didn't understand anything. All she could do was try to finish what she'd come here for.

Action, that was what she needed. Thought could wait. It would have to wait.

Then she glanced at the wharf.

She couldn't believe it. It seemed as if at least a week had passed since she yelled at Daphne, *and they were all still here.*

The boats were here, the girls were here, and Daphne was running toward her.

Rashel strode to meet her. She grabbed Daphne by the shoulders and shook hard.

"Get—out—of—here! Do you *understand*? What do I have to do, throw you in the water?"

Daphne's eyes were huge and blue. Her blond hair flew like thistledown with the shaking. When Rashel stopped, she gasped, "But you can come with us now!"

"No, I can't! I still have things to do."

"Like what?" Then Daphne's eyes darted to the cliff. She stared at Rashel. "You're going *after* them? You're crazy!" Looking frightened, she grabbed Rashel's hands on her shoulders. "Rashel, there are supposed to be eight of them, right? Plus Lily and Ivan and who knows what else! You really think you can kill them all? What, are they all just going to line up?"

"No. I don't know. But I don't need to kill them all. If I can get the guy who set this up, the client, it will be worth it."

Daphne was shaking her head, in tears. "It won't be worth it! Not if they kill you—which they will. You're already hurt—"

"It'll be worth it if I can stop him from doing this again," Rashel said quietly. She couldn't yell anymore. She didn't have the strength. Her voice was quenched, but she held Daphne's eyes. "Now get somebody to throw me some rope or something to tie these guys with. And then leave. No, give me five minutes to get to the top of the cliff. Six minutes. That way maybe I can surprise them before they realize you're gone."

Daphne was crying steadily now. Before she could say anything, Rashel went on. "Daphne, any minute now they *could* realize that. Someone's bound to check the cellar before midnight. Every second we stand here could make the difference. Please, please, don't fight me anymore."

Daphne opened her mouth, then shut it. Her eyes were desolate. "Please try to take care of yourself," she whispered. She let go of Rashel's shoulders and hugged her hard. "We all know you're doing it for us. I'm proud to be your friend."

Then she turned and ran, herding the others toward the boats.

A moment later she threw Rashel two pieces of line. Rashel tied up Quinn first, then the werewolf.

"Six minutes," she said to Daphne. Daphne nodded, trying not to cry.

Rashel wouldn't say goodbye. She hated that. Even though she knew perfectly well that she was never going to see Daphne again.

Without looking back, she loped up the hiking trail.

CHAPTER 14

The first person Rashel met in the mansion was Ivan. It was sheer dumb luck, the same luck that had helped keep her alive so far tonight. She slipped in the back door, the way she and the girls had gone out. Standing in the huge silent kitchen, she listened for an instant to the music that was still blasting from the inner house.

Then she swiveled to check the cellar—and met Ivan the Terrible running up the stairs.

He had clearly just discovered that his twenty-four valuable slave girls were missing. His blond hair was flying, his eyes were wide with alarm, his mouth was twisted. He had the taser in one hand and a bunch of plastic handcuffs—the kind police use on rioters—in the other.

When Rashel suddenly appeared on the stairway, his eyes flew open even wider. His mouth opened in astonishment—and then Rashel's foot impacted with his forehead. The snap kick knocked him backward, and he tumbled down the stairs to hit the wooden door below.

Rashel leaped after him, making it to the bottom only a second after he did. But he was already out.

"What are these? Were you supposed to take some girls up?" She kicked at the plastic handcuffs. Ivan the Unconscious didn't answer.

She glanced at her watch. Only a quarter to nine. Maybe he'd been taking the girls to get washed or something. It seemed too early to start the feast.

Running noiselessly back up the stairs, she quietly closed the door. Now she had to follow the music. She needed to see where the vampires were, how they were situated, how she could best get at them. She wondered where Lily was.

The kitchen opened into a grand dining room with an enormous built-in sideboard. It had undoubtedly been made to accommodate whole suckling pigs or something, but Rashel had a dreadful vision of a girl lying on that coffinlike mahogany shelf, hands tied behind her, while vampire after vampire stopped by to have a snack.

She pushed the idea out of her mind and moved silently across the floorboards.

The dining room led to a hall, and it was from the end of the hallway that music was coming. Rashel slipped into the dimly lit hall like a shadow, moving closer and closer to the doors there. The last door was the only one that showed light.

That one, she thought.

Before she could get near it, a figure blocked the light. Instantly Rashel darted through the nearest doorway.

She held her breath, standing in the darkened room, watching the hall. If only one or two vampires came out, she could pick them off.

But nobody came out and she realized it must have just been someone passing in front of the light. At the same moment she realized that the music was very loud.

This wasn't another room—it was the same room. She was in one gigantic double parlor, with a huge wooden screen breaking it up into two separate spaces. The screen was solid, but carved into a lacy pattern that let flickering light through.

Rashel thrust her knife in her waistband, then crept to the screen and applied her eye.

A spacious room, very masculine, paneled like the dining room in mahogany and floored in cherry parquet. Glass brick windows—opaque. All Rashel's worry about somebody looking out had been for nothing. A fire burned in a massive fireplace, the light bringing out the ruddy tones in the wood. The whole room looked red and secret.

And there they were. The vampires for the bloodfeast.

Seven of the most powerful made vampires in the world, Fayth had said. Rashel counted heads swiftly. Yes, seven. No Lily.

"You boys don't look that scary," she murmured.

That was one thing about made vampires. Unlike the

lamia, who could stop aging—or start again—whenever they wanted, made vampires were stuck. And since the process of turning a human body into a vampire body was incredibly difficult, only a young human could survive it.

Try to turn somebody over twenty into a vampire and they would burn out. Fry. Die.

The result was that all made vampires were stuck as teenagers.

What Rashel was looking at could have been the cast for some new TV soap about friends. Seven teenage guys, different sizes, different colors, but all Hollywood handsome, and all dressed to kill. They could have been talking and laughing about a fishing trip or a school dance . . . except for their eyes.

That was what gave them away, Rashel thought. The eyes showed a depth no high school guy could ever have. An experience, an intelligence . . . and a coldness.

Some of these teenagers were undoubtedly hundreds of years old, maybe thousands. All of them were absolutely deadly.

Or else they wouldn't be here. They each expected to kill three innocent girls starting at midnight.

These thoughts flashed through Rashel's mind in a matter of seconds. She had already decided on the best way to plunge into the room and start the attack. But one thing kept her from doing it.

There were only seven vampires. And the eighth was the one she wanted. The client. The one who'd hired Quinn and set up the feast.

Maybe it *was* one of these. Maybe that tall one with the dark skin and the look of authority. Or the silvery blond with the odd smile. . . .

No. Nobody really looks like a host. I think it's the one who's still missing.

But maybe she couldn't afford to wait. They might hear the powerboats leaving over the steady pounding of the music. Maybe she should just . . .

Something grabbed her from behind.

This time she had no warning. And she wasn't surprised anymore. Her opinion of herself as a warrior had plummeted.

She intended to fight, though. She went limp to loosen the grip, then reached between her own legs to grab her attacker's ankle. A jerk up would throw him off balance. . . .

Don't do it. I don't want to have to stun you, but I will.

Quinn.

She recognized the mental voice, and the hand clamped across her mouth. And both the telepathy and the skin contact were having an effect on her.

It wasn't like before; no lightning bolts, no explosions. But she was overwhelmed with a sense of *Quinn.* She seemed to feel his mind—and the feeling was one of drowning in dark chaos. A storm that seemed just as likely to kill Quinn as anyone else.

He lifted her cleanly and backed out of the room with her, into the hall, then up a flight of stairs. Rashel didn't fight. She tried to clear her head and wait for an opportunity.

By the time he'd pulled her into an upstairs room and shut the door, she realized that there wasn't going to be an opportunity.

He was just too strong, and he could stun her telepathically the instant she moved to get away. The tables had turned. There was nothing to do now but hope that she could face death as calmly as he had. At least, she thought, it would put a stop to her confusion.

He let go of her and she slowly turned to look at him.

What she saw sent chills between her shoulder blades. His eyes were as dark and chaotic as the clouds she'd sensed in his mind. It was scarier than the cold hunger she'd seen in the eyes of the seven guys downstairs.

Then he smiled.

A smile that shed rainbows. Rashel pressed her back against the wall and tried to brace herself.

"Give me the knife."

She simply looked at him. He pulled it out of her waistband and tossed it on the bed.

"I don't like being knocked out," he said. "I don't know why, but something about it really bothers me."

"Quinn, just get it over with."

"And it took me a while to get myself untied. Every time I meet you, I seem to end up hog-tied and unconscious. It's getting monotonous."

"Quinn . . . you're a vampire. I'm a vampire hunter. Do what you have to."

"We're also always threatening each other. Have you noticed that? Of course, everything we keep saying is true. It *is* kill or be killed. And you've killed a lot of my people, Rashel the Cat."

"And you've killed a lot of mine, John Quinn."

He glanced away, looking into a middle distance. His pupils were enormous. "Less than you might think, actually. I don't usually kill to feed. But, yes, I've done enough. I said before, I know what you think of me."

Rashel said nothing. She was frightened and confused and had been under strain for quite a long time. She felt that at any moment she could snap.

"We belong to two different races, races that hate each other. There's no way to get around that." He turned his dark eyes back on her and gave her a brilliant smile. "Unless, of course, we *change* it."

"What are you talking about?"

"I'm going to make you a vampire."

Something inside Rashel seemed to give way and fall. She felt as if her legs might collapse.

He couldn't mean it, he couldn't be serious. But he was. She could tell. There was a kind of surface serenity pasted over the dark roiling clouds in his eyes.

So this was how he'd solved an unsolvable problem. He *had* snapped.

Rashel whispered, "You know you can't do that."

"I know I *can* do that. It's very simple, actually—all we have to do is exchange blood. And it's the only way." He took hold of her arms just above the elbow. "Don't you understand? As long as you're human, Night World law says you have to *die* if I love you."

Rashel stood stricken.

Quinn had stopped short, as if he were startled himself by what he'd said. Then he gave an odd laugh and shook his head. "If I love you," he repeated. "And that's the problem, of course. I do love you."

Rashel leaned against the wall for support. She couldn't think anymore. She couldn't even breathe properly. And somewhere deep inside her there was a trembling that wouldn't stop.

"I've loved you from that first night, Rashel the Cat. I didn't want to admit it, but it was true." He was still gripping her tightly by the arms, leaning close to her, but his eyes were distant, lost in the past.

"I'd never met a human like you," he said softly, as if remembering. "You were strong, you weren't weak and pathetic. You weren't looking for your own destruction. But you were going to let me go. Strength *and* compassion. And . . . honor. Of course I loved you." His dark eyes focused again. He looked at her sharply. "I'd have been crazy not to."

Falling into darkness . . . Rashel had a terrifying desire to simply collapse in his arms. Give in. He was so strangely beautiful, and the power of his personality was overwhelming.

And of course she loved him, too.

That was suddenly excruciatingly clear. Undeniable. From the beginning he had struck a chord in her that no one else had ever touched. He was so much like her—a hunter, a fighter. But he had honor, too. However he might try to deny it or get around it, deep inside him there was still honor.

And like her, he knew the dark side of life, the pain, the violence. They had both seen—and done—things that normal people wouldn't understand.

She was supposed to hate him . . . but from the beginning she'd seen herself in him. She had felt the bond, the connection between them. . . .

Rashel shook her head. "No!" She had to stop thinking these things. She would *not* surrender to the darkness.

"You can't stop me, you know," Quinn said softly. "That ought to make things easier for you. You don't even have to make a decision. It's all my fault. I'm very, very bad, and I'm going to make you a vampire."

Somehow that gave Rashel her voice back. "How can you do that—to someone you *love*?" she spat.

"Because I don't want you dead! Because as long as you're human, you're going to get yourself killed!" He put his face close to hers, their foreheads almost touching. "I will *not* let you kill yourself," he said through his teeth.

"If you make me a vampire, I *will* kill myself," Rashel said.

Her mind had cleared. However much she wanted to give in, however enticing the darkness might be, it all disappeared when she thought of how it would end. She would be a vampire. She'd be driven by bloodlust to do things that would horrify her right now. And she'd undoubtedly find excuses for doing them. She would become a monster.

Quinn was looking shaken. She'd scared him, she could see it in his eyes.

"You'll feel differently once it's done," he said.

"No. Listen to me, Quinn." She kept her eyes on his, looking deep, trying to let him see the truth of what she was saying. "If you make me a vampire, the moment I wake up I'll stab myself with my own knife. Do you think I'm not brave enough?"

"You're too brave; that's your problem." He was faltering. The surface serenity was breaking up. But that wasn't really helpful, Rashel realized, because underneath it was an agony of desperate confusion. Quinn really couldn't see any other solution. Rashel couldn't see any herself—except that she didn't really expect to survive tonight.

Quinn's face hardened, and she could see him pushing away doubts. "You'll get used to it," he said harshly, his voice grating. "You'll see. Let's start now," he added.

And then he bit her.

He was so fast. Unbelievably fast. He caught her jaw and tilted her head back and to the side—not roughly but with

an irresistible control and precision. Then before Rashel had
time to scream, she felt a hot sting. She felt teeth, vampire
teeth, extended to an impossible delicacy and sharpness,
pierce her flesh.

This is it. This is death.

Panic flooded her. But it wasn't death, of course—not
yet. She wouldn't even be changed into a vampire by a single
exchange of blood. No, instead it would be slow torture . . .
days of agony . . . pain. . . .

She kept waiting for the pain.

Instead she felt a strange warmth and languor. Was he actually drinking her blood? All she could sense was Quinn's mouth
nuzzling at her neck, his arms around her tightly. And . . .

His mind.

It happened all at once. In a sudden silent explosion, white
light engulfed her. It burst around her. She was floating in
it. Quinn was floating in it. It was shining around them and
through them, and she could feel a connection with Quinn
that made their last connection seem like a faulty telephone
line.

She *knew* him. She could see him, his soul, whatever you
wanted to call it, whatever it was that made him John Quinn.
They seemed to be floating together in some other space, in a
naked white light that revealed everything and mercilessly lit
up all the most secret places.

And if anyone had asked her, Rashel would have said that

would be horrible, and she would have run for her life to get away from it.

But it wasn't horrible. She could see dreadful dark bits in Quinn's mind, and dreadful dark bits in hers. Tangled, thorny, scary parts, full of anger and hate. But there were so many other parts—some of them almost unused—that were beautiful and strong and whole. There was so much *potential.* Rainbow places that were aching to grow. Other parts that seemed to quiver with light, desperate to be awakened.

We ask so little of ourselves, Rashel thought in wonder. If everybody's like this—we stunt ourselves so badly. We could be so much more. . . .

I don't want you to be more. You're amazing enough the way you are.

It was Quinn. Not even his voice, just—Quinn. His thoughts. And Rashel knew her thoughts flowed to him without her even making an effort.

You know what I mean. Isn't this strange? Does this always happen with vampires?

Nothing like this has ever happened to me in my life, Quinn said.

What he felt was even more, and Rashel could sense it directly, in a dizzying sweet wave. There was an understanding between them that ran deeper than any words could convey.

Whatever was happening to them, however they had gotten to this place, one thing was obvious. Under the white light that revealed their inner selves, it was clear that small differences like being vampire or human didn't matter. They were both just people. John Quinn and Rashel Jordan. People who were stumbling through life trying to deal with the hurt.

Because there was hurt. There was pain in the landscape of Quinn's mind. Rashel sensed it without words or even images; she could *feel* the feelings that had scarred Quinn.

Your father did something—he killed Dove? Oh, John. Oh, John, I'm so sorry. I didn't know.

Rainbow lights shimmered when she called him John. It was the part of him that he had repressed the most ruthlessly. The part that she could almost feel growing in her presence.

No wonder you hated humans. After everything you'd been through, to have your own father want you dead . . .

And no wonder you hated vampires. They killed someone close to you—your mother? And you were so young. I'm . . . sorry. He wasn't as easy with words as she was, but here they didn't need words. She could sense his sorrow, his shame, and his fierce protectiveness. And she could sense the emotion behind his next question. *Who did it?*

I don't know. I'll probably never know. Rashel didn't want to pursue it. She didn't want to feed the dark side of Quinn; she wanted to see more of the shimmering light. She wanted to make the light grow until the dark disappeared.

Rashel, that may not be possible. Quinn's thought wasn't

bitter; it was serious and gentle. Tinged with infinite regret. *I may not be able to become anything better—*

Of course you can. We all can. Rashel cut him off with absolute determination. She could feel the bone-deep cold that had set into him years ago, that he'd allowed to set in. *I won't let you be cold,* she told him, and she went for a romp in his mind, kissing things and blowing warmth into them, thinking sunlight and comfort everywhere.

Please stop; I think you're killing me. Quinn's thought was shaky—half serious and half hysterical, like the helpless gasp of somebody being tickled to death.

Rashel's whole being was singing with elation. She was young—how strange that she had never really *felt* young until now—and she was in love and stronger than she had ever been before. She had John Quinn the Vampire squirming and semi-hysterical. She was unstoppable. Anything was possible.

I'll make *everything be right,* she told Quinn, and she was happy to see that she'd driven his doubt and his sadness away, at least for the moment. *Do you really want me to stop?*

No. Quinn sounded dazed now—and bemused. *I've decided I'll enjoy dying this way. But . . .*

Rashel couldn't follow the rest of his thought, but she felt a new coldness, something like a wind from outside.

Outside.

She'd forgotten there was an outside. In here, in the private cocoon of their minds, there was nothing but her and Quinn. It was almost as if nothing else existed.

But . . .

There was a whole world out there. Other people. Things happening. Things Rashel had to stop. . . .

"Oh, God, Quinn—the vampires."

CHAPTER 15

The sound of her own voice sent Rashel spinning out of the light.

It was as if she were emerging from deep water—from one world into another. Or as if she were re-entering her own body. For a moment everything was confusion, and Rashel wasn't sure of where she was or how she was positioned . . . and then she felt her arms and legs and saw yellow light. Lamplight. She was in an upstairs room in a mansion on a private island, and Quinn was holding her.

They had somehow ended up on the floor, half kneeling, half supported by the wall, their arms around each other, Rashel's head on his shoulder. She had no idea when he'd stopped biting her. She also had no idea how much time had passed.

She coughed a little, shaken by what had just happened. That other place, with the light—it still seemed more real than the hard shiny boards of the floor underneath her and the white walls of the room. But it also seemed encased in its own reality. Like a dream. She didn't know if they would ever be able to get back there again.

"Quinn?" He was Quinn again. Not John.

"Yes."

"Do you know what happened? I mean, do you understand it?"

"I think," he said, and his voice was gentle and precise, "that sharing blood can strengthen a telepathic bond. I've always been able to block it out when I fed before, but . . ." He didn't finish.

"But it happened that other time. Or something like it happened. When I first met you."

"Yes. Well. Well, I think it's . . . there's something called . . ." He gave up and resorted to nonverbal communication. *There's something called the soulmate principle. I've never believed in it. I've laughed at people who talked about it. I would have bet my life that—*

"What *is* it, Quinn?" Rashel had heard of it, too, especially recently. But it wasn't something from her world, and she wanted a Night Person to explain.

It's the idea that everyone has one and just one soulmate in the world, and that if you find them, you recognize them immediately. And . . . well, that's that.

"But it's not supposed to happen between humans and Night People. Right?"

There are some people who think that it is happening—now—for some reason—especially between humans and Night People. The Redferns seem to be getting it in particular. There was a pause, then Quinn said aloud, "I should probably apologize to some of them, actually." He sounded bemused.

Rashel sat up, which was difficult. She didn't want to let go of Quinn. He kept hold of her fingers, which helped a little.

He looked more mussed than he had down near the wharf, his neat hair disordered, his eyes large and dark and dazed. She met his gaze directly. "You think we're soulmates?"

"Well." He blinked. "Do you have a better explanation?"

"No." She took a breath. "Do you still want to make me a vampire?"

He stared at her, and something flamed and then fell in pain in his eyes. For an instant he looked as if she'd hit him—then all she could see was regret.

"Oh, Rashel." In one motion he caught her and held her. His face was pressed to her hair. She could feel him breathing like some stricken creature—and then she felt him regain control, grabbing discipline from somewhere, wrapping himself in it. He rested his chin on her head. "I'm sorry you have to ask that, but I understand. I don't want to make you a vampire. I want—" *I want you to be what you were two minutes ago. That happy, that idealistic. . . .*

He sounded as if it were something that had been lost forever.

But Rashel felt a new happiness, and a new confidence. He had changed. She could sense how much he had changed already. They were in the real world, and he wasn't raving about needing to kill her, or her needing to kill him.

"I just wanted to be sure," she said. She tightened her own arms around him. "I don't know what's going to happen—but as long as we're right together, I think I can face it."

I think we live or die together from now on, Quinn said simply.

Yes, Rashel thought. She could still feel lingering sadness in Quinn, and confusion in herself, but they *were* right together. She didn't need to doubt him anymore.

They trusted each other.

"We have to do something about the people downstairs," she said.

"Yes."

"But we can't kill them."

"No. There's been enough killing. It has to stop." Quinn sounded like a swimmer who'd been tumbling in a riptide, and whose feet had finally found solid ground.

Rashel sat up to look at him. "But we can't just let them walk out of here. What if they try it again? I mean, whoever set this bloodfeast up . . ." She suddenly realized that she had asked everybody else, but not him. "Quinn, who *did* set this up?"

He smiled, a faint echo of his old savage smile. Now it was grim and self-mocking. "I don't know."

"You don't *know*?"

"Some vampire who wanted to get the made vampires together. But I've never met him. Lily was the go-between, but I'm not sure she knows either. She only spoke to him on the phone. Neither of us asked a lot of questions. We were doing it for the money." He said it flatly, not sparing himself.

And to be rebellious, Rashel thought. To be as bad and as damned as possible, because you figured you might as well. She said, "Whoever it is might just go somewhere else and find somebody else to get his slaves for him. Those seven guys could be having a new bloodfeast next month."

"That has to be stopped, too," Quinn said. "How to stop it without violence, that's the question." His fingers were still tight on Rashel's, but he was staring into the distance, lost in grim and competent thought.

It was a new side of Quinn. Rashel had seen him in almost every mood from despairing to manic, but she had never *worked* with him before. Now she realized that he was going to make a strong and resourceful ally.

Suddenly Quinn seemed to focus.

"I've got it," he said. He smiled suddenly, mocking but without the bitterness. "When violence won't work, there's no other choice but to try persuasion."

"That's not funny."

"It's not meant to be."

"You're going to say, 'Please don't kill any more young girls'?"

"I'm going to say, 'Please don't kill any more young girls or I'll report you to the Joint Council.' Listen, Rashel." He took her by the arms, his eyes flashing with excitement. "I have some authority in the Night World—I'm the Redfern heir. And Hunter Redfern has more. Between us, we can make all kinds of trouble for these made vampires."

"But Fayth—a friend of mine—said they were all so powerful." In the intensity of the moment, Rashel almost missed the fact that she'd just called Fayth her friend.

Quinn was shaking his head. "No, you have to understand. These aren't rogues, they're Night World citizens. And what they're doing is completely illegal. You can't just kill a bunch of girls from one area without permission. Slavery's illegal, blood-feasts are illegal. And no matter how powerful they are, they can't stand up against the Night World Council."

"But—"

"We threaten them with exposure to the Council. With exposure to Hunter Redfern—and to the lamia. The lamia will go crazy at the thought of made vampires getting together in some kind of alliance. They'll take it as a threat of civil war."

It might work, Rashel was thinking. The made vampires were just individuals—they'd be up against whole lamia families. Especially against the Redfern family, the oldest and most respected clan of vampires.

"Everybody's scared of Hunter Redfern," she said slowly.

"He's got tremendous influence. He practically owns the Council. He could run them out of the Night World if he wanted. I think they'll listen."

"You really do think of him as a father, don't you?" Rashel said, her voice soft. She searched Quinn's eyes. "Whatever you say about hating him—you respect him."

"He's not as bad as most. He has . . . honor, I guess. Usually."

And he's a New Englander, Rashel thought. That means he's against vice. She considered another moment, then she nodded. Her heart was beating fast, but she could feel a smile breaking on her face. "Let's try persuasion."

They stood—and then they paused a moment, looking at each other. We're strong, Rashel thought. We've got unity. If anyone can do this, we can.

She picked up her knife almost absentmindedly. It was a piece of art, a valued possession, and she didn't want to lose it.

They walked down the stairs side by side. Music was still blasting from the gathering room at the end of the hall. It hadn't been that long, Rashel realized. The whole world had changed since she'd been in this hallway—but somehow it had all happened in minutes.

Now, Quinn said silently before they went in. *There shouldn't be any danger—I don't think they'll be stupid enough to attack me—but be alert anyway.*

Rashel nodded. She felt cool and businesslike, and she thought she was perfectly rational. It was only later that she realized they had walked into the room like little lambs into the tiger's lair, still dizzy and reeling from the discovery of love.

Quinn went in first and she could hear voices stop as he did. Then she was walking through the door, into that ruddy flickering room with shadows dancing on the walls.

And there they were again, those handsome young guys who looked like a TV-series ensemble. They were looking at Quinn with various expressions of interest and surprise. When they saw her, the expressions sharpened to pleasure and inquiry.

"Hey, Quinn!"

"Hi there, Quinn."

"So you've arrived at last. You've kept us waiting long enough." That from the dark one who was looking at his watch.

Quinn said, "Turn off the music."

Someone went to a built-in mahogany cabinet and turned off an expensive stereo.

Quinn was looking around the room, as if to appraise each of them. "Campbell," he said, nodding slightly. "Radhu. Azarius. Max."

"So you're the one who brought us here," Campbell said. He had rusty hair and a sleepy smile. "We've all been dying to find out."

"Who's that?" someone else added, peering at Rashel. "The first course?"

Quinn smiled fractionally, with a look that made the guy who'd asked step backward. "No, she's not the first course," he said softly. "In fact, unfortunately, all the courses have disappeared."

There was a silence. Everyone stared at him. Then the guy with the silver-blond hair said, *"What?"*

"They've all—*fsst*—disappeared." Quinn made an expressive gesture. "Escaped. Vanished."

Another silence. Rashel didn't like this one. She was beginning to get an odd impression from the group, as if she were in a room, not with people, but with animals that had been kept past their feeding time.

"What the hell are you talking about?" the dark one, the one Quinn had called Azarius, said tightly.

"What kind of joke is this?" Campbell added.

"It's not a joke. The girls who were brought for the blood-feast are gone," Quinn said slowly and distinctly, just in case anybody hadn't gotten it yet. Then he said, "And as a matter of fact, it's a good thing."

"A *good* thing? Quinn, we're starving."

"They can't have gone *too* far," the silver blond said. "After all, it's an island. Let's go and—"

"Nobody's going anywhere," Quinn said. Rashel moved closer to him. She was still nervous. These guys were on the edge of getting out of control.

But she trusted Quinn, and she could tell they were afraid of him. And, she told herself, they'll be even more afraid in a minute.

"Look, Quinn, if you brought us here to—"

"I didn't bring you here. In fact, I don't know *who* brought you here, but it doesn't matter. I've got the same thing to say to all of you. There isn't going to be any bloodfeast, now or ever. And anybody who objects to that can take their problem to the Council."

That shut everyone up. They simply stared at Quinn. It was clearly the last thing they expected.

"In fact, if you don't want the Council to hear about this, I'd advise everybody to go home quietly and pretend it never happened. And to have a headache the next time anybody asks you to a bloodfeast."

This silence was broken by somebody muttering, "You dirty . . ."

Meanwhile, Rashel's mind had begun to tick. Just *how* were these guys going to go home quietly? There weren't any boats. Unless the host brought one when he came—*if* he came. And where was he, anyway? And where was Lily?

"Quinn," she said softly.

But somebody else was speaking. "You'd tell the Council?" a lean tough-looking guy with brown hair asked.

"No, I'd let Hunter Redfern tell the Council," Quinn said. "And I don't really think you want that. He might put it in a bad light. Raise your hands everybody who thinks Hunter Redfern would approve of this little party."

"Do I get a vote?"

The voice came from the doorway. It was deeper than the voices of the young guys in the room. Rashel recognized the sound of danger instinctively, and turned. And later it seemed to her that even before she turned, she knew what she would see.

A tall man standing easily, with a girl and a child behind him in the shadows. He was colored by the flickering ruby light of the fire, but Rashel could still see that his hair was red as blood. And his eyes were golden.

Golden like hawk's eyes, like amber. Like Lily Redfern's eyes. Why hadn't she realized that before?

The face was a face she would never forget. It came to her every night in her dreams. It was the man who'd killed her mother. The man who'd chased her through the climbing structure, promising her ice cream.

All at once, Rashel was five years old again, weak and helpless and terrified.

"Hello, Quinn," Hunter Redfern said.

Quinn was absolutely still beside Rashel. She had the feeling that he couldn't even think. And she understood why. She'd seen into his mind; she knew what Hunter represented to him. Stern necessity, even ruthlessness, but honor, too. And he was just now finding out that that was all a lie.

"Don't look so upset," Hunter said. He stepped forward with an amiable smile. His golden eyes were fixed on Quinn; he hadn't even glanced at Rashel yet. "There's a reason for all this." He gestured to the vampires in the room, and his voice was gentle, rational. "We need allies in the Council; the lamia are getting too lax. Once I've explained it all to you, you'll understand."

The way he'd made Quinn understand that Quinn had to be a vampire, Rashel thought. The way he'd made Quinn understand that humans were the enemy.

She was shaking all over, but there was a white-hot fire inside her that burned through the fear.

"Was there a reason for killing my mother?" she said.

The golden eyes turned toward her. Hunter looked mildly startled. Beside her, Quinn's head jerked around.

"I was only five, but I remember it all," Rashel said. She took a step closer to Hunter. "You killed her just like *that*—snapped her neck. Was there a reason for killing Timmy? He was four years old and you drank his blood. Was there a reason for killing my great-aunt? You set a fire to get me, but it got her."

She stopped, staring into those predatory golden eyes. She'd searched for this man for twelve years, and now he didn't seem to recognize her. "What's wrong, did you hunt too many little kids to keep track of?" she said. "Or are you so crazy you believe your own public image?"

Quinn whispered, "Rashel . . ."

She turned. "I'm sure. He was the one."

In that instant, she saw Quinn's face harden implacably against the man who'd made him a Redfern. His eyes went dark as black holes—no light escaped. Rashel suddenly had the feeling of glacial cold. Look into eyes like that and what you saw alone might kill you, she thought.

But she had her own fire inside her, her own vengeance. The knife was in her waistband. If she could just get close enough. . . . She moved toward Hunter Redfern again. "You destroyed my life. And you don't even remember, do you?"

"I remember," the little shadow beside him said.

And then the world flipped and Rashel felt the floor slipping away from her. The child behind Hunter was walking into the light—and suddenly she could smell plastic and old socks, and she could feel vinyl under her hands. Memories were flooding up so quickly that she was drowning in them.

All she could say was "Oh, Timmy. Oh, God, Timmy."

He was standing there, just as she'd seen him last, twelve years ago. Shiny dark hair and wide tilted blue eyes. Except that the eyes weren't exactly a child's eyes. They were some strange and terrible combination of child and adult. There was too much knowledge in them.

"You left me," Timmy said. "You didn't care about me."

Rashel sank her teeth into her lip, but tears spilled anyway. "I'm sorry . . ."

"Nobody cared about me," Timmy said. He reached up to take Hunter's sleeve. "No humans, anyway. Humans are vermin." He smiled his old sweet smile.

Hunter looked down at Timmy, then up at Quinn. "It's amazing how quickly they learn. You haven't met Timmy, have you? He's been living in Vegas, but I think he can be useful here." He turned to Rashel and his eyes were pure evil. "Of course I remember you. It's just that you've changed a little; you've gotten older. You're different from us, you see."

"You're weak," Lily put in. She had stepped forward, too, to stand beside her father. Now she linked her arm in his. "You're short-lived. You're not very bright, and not very important. In a word, you're . . . *dinner.*"

Hunter smiled. "Well put." Then he dropped the smile and said to Quinn, "Step away from her, son."

Quinn moved slightly, closer to Rashel. "This is my soul-mate," he said, in his softest and most disturbing voice. "And we're leaving together."

Hunter Redfern stared at him for several long moments. Something like disbelief flickered in his eyes. Then he recovered and said quietly, "What a shame."

Behind Rashel there were noises of stirring. It was as if a hot wind from the savanna had blown in, and the lions had caught its scent.

"You know, I was already worried about you, Quinn," Hunter said. "Last summer you let Ash and his sisters get away with running out on the enclave. Don't think I didn't notice that. You're getting lax, getting soft. There's too much of that going around lately."

Stand back to back, Quinn told Rashel. She was already moving into position. The vampires were forming a ring, encircling them. She could see smiles on every face.

"And Lily says you've been strange these last few days—moody. She said you seemed preoccupied with a human girl."

Rashel drew her knife. The vampires were watching her with the fixed attention of big felines watching their prey. Absolute focus.

"But the soulmate idea—that's really the last straw. It's like a disease infecting our people. You understand why I have to stamp it out." Hunter paused. "For old time's sake, let's finish this quickly."

A voice that wasn't Quinn's added in Rashel's mind, *I told you I'd see you later.*

Rashel stood on the balls of her feet, letting Hunter's words slide off her and drip away. She couldn't think about him right now. She had to concentrate on awareness, open her energy, and free her mind. This was going to be the biggest fight of her life, and she needed *zanshin.*

But even as she found it, a small voice inside her was whispering the truth. There were simply too many vampires. She and Quinn couldn't hold them all off at once.

CHAPTER 16

A fighter knows instinctively when there's no chance.
But Rashel planned to fight anyway.

And then she noticed something wrong.

The vampires should have caught it first. Their senses were sharper. But their senses were turned inward, focused on the victims in front of them. Rashel was the only one whose senses were turned outward, alert to everything but focused on nothing.

There was a smell that was wrong and a sound. The smell was sharp, stinging, and close by. The sound was soft, distant, but recognizable.

Gasoline. She could smell gasoline. And she could hear a faint dull roar that sounded like the fireplace in the gathering room—but was coming from somewhere else in the house.

It didn't make sense. She didn't understand. But she believed it.

"Quinn, get ready to run," she said, a gasp on a soft breath. Something was about to happen.

No, we have to fight—

His thought to her broke off. Rashel turned to look at the doorway.

Hunter Redfern had moved into the gathering room—but there was *someone* in the hall. Then the someone stepped forward and Rashel could see her face.

Nyala was smiling brilliantly. Her small queenly head was high and her dark eyes were flashing. She was holding a red gasoline can in one hand and a liter of grapefruit juice in the other. The bottle was almost full of liquid and had a burning rag stuffed in the top.

Gas. Gas from the pump on the wharf, Rashel thought. A Generation-X Molotov cocktail.

"It's all over the house," Nyala said, and her voice was lilting. "Gallons and gallons. All over the rooms and the doors."

But she shouldn't be hanging *on* to it, Rashel thought. That bottle is going to explode.

"You see, I *am* a real vampire hunter, Rashel. I figure this way, we get rid of them all at once."

And the house is already burning. . . .

Behind the carved screen on the right side of the room, ruddy light was flickering, growing. The faint roar that had disturbed Rashel was louder now. Closer.

And everything's *wood,* Rashel thought. Wood paneling,

wood floors. Frame house. A deathtrap for vampires.

"Get her," Hunter Redfern said. But none of the vampires charged toward Nyala with her about-to-explode bottle of death and her can of fire accelerant. In fact, they were backing away, moving to the perimeter of the room.

Hunter spun to face Nyala directly. *You need to put that down,* he began in telepathic tones of absolute authority—at the same time Rashel shouted, "Nyala, *no*—"

The sound of telepathy seemed to set something off in Nyala. Flashing a dazzling savage smile, she smashed the grapefruit juice bottle at his feet.

With almost the same motion, she threw the gasoline can, too. It was flying in a graceful arc toward the fireplace, spinning, spilling liquid, and vampires were scattering to try to get out of the way.

And then everything was exploding—or maybe *erupting* was a better word. It was as if a dragon had breathed suddenly into the room, sending a roaring gale of fire through it.

But Rashel didn't have time to watch—she and Quinn were both diving. Quinn was diving for the floor past Nyala, trying to drag Rashel with him. Rashel was diving for Timmy.

She didn't know why. She didn't think about it consciously. She simply had to do it.

She hit Timmy with the entire force of her body and knocked him to the floor. She covered him as the fire erupted behind her. Then she scrambled to her knees, her arm locked around his chest.

Everything was noise and heat and confusion. Vampires were yelling at each other, running, shoving each other. The ones who'd been splattered with gas were on fire, trying to put it out, getting in one another's way.

"Come on!" Quinn said, pulling Rashel up. "I know a way outside."

Rashel looked for Nyala. She didn't see her. As Quinn dragged her into the hall, she saw dark smoke come billowing from the dining-room area. The hall was bathed in reddish light.

"Come on!"

Quinn was pulling her across the hall, through the smoke. Into a room that was full of orange flames.

"Quinn—"

Timmy was kicking and struggling in Rashel's arms. Yelling at her. She kept her grip on him.

And she went with Quinn. She had to trust him. He knew the house.

She hadn't realized how frightening fire was, though. It was like a beast with hot shriveling breath. It seemed *alive* and it seemed to want to get her, roaring out at her from unexpected places.

And it spread so fast. Rashel would never have believed it could move so quickly through a house, even a house soaked with gasoline. In a matter of minutes the building had become an inferno. Everywhere she looked, there was fire, smoke, and a horrifying reflection of flames.

They were on the other side of the room now, and Quinn was kicking at a door. His sleeve was on fire. Rashel twisted her hand out of his and beat at it to put it out. She almost lost hold of Timmy.

Then the door was swinging outward and cool air was rushing in and the fire was roaring like a crazy thing to meet it. She was simply running, in panic, her only thought to hold on to Timmy and to stay with Quinn.

They were out. But she smelled burning. And now Quinn was grabbing her, rolling her over and over on the sandy unpaved road. Rashel realized, dimly, that her clothes were on fire in back.

Quinn stopped rolling her. Rashel sat up, tried to glance at her own back, then looked for Timmy.

He was crouched on the road, staring at the house. Rashel could see flames coming out of the windows. Smoke was pouring upward and everything seemed as bright as daylight beneath it.

"Are you all right?" Quinn said urgently. He was looking her over.

Rashel's whole body was washed with adrenaline and her heart was pounding insanely. But she couldn't take her eyes off the house.

She stumbled to her feet. "Nyala's in there! I have to get her."

Quinn looked at her as if she were raving. Rashel just shook her head and started helplessly toward the house. She didn't want to go anywhere near it. She knew the fire wanted her dead. But she couldn't leave Nyala in there to burn.

Then Quinn was shoving her roughly back. "You stay here. I'll get her."

"No! I have to—"

"You have to watch Timmy! Look, he's getting away!"

Rashel whirled. She didn't have any clear idea of where Timmy might be getting away to—but he was on his feet and moving. Toward the house, then away from it. She grabbed for him again. When she turned back toward Quinn, Quinn was gone.

No—there he was, darting into the house. Timmy was screaming again, kicking in her arms.

"I hate you!" he shouted. "Let go of me! Why did you take me out?"

Rashel stared at the house. Quinn was inside now. In that holocaust of flame. And he'd gone because of her, to save her from going herself.

Please, she thought suddenly and distinctly. Please don't let him die.

The flames were roaring higher. The night was brilliant with them. Fire was raining in little burning bits from the sky, and Rashel's nose and eyes stung. She knew she should get farther back, but she couldn't. She had to watch for Quinn.

"Why? I hate you! Why did you take me out?"

Rashel looked at the strange little creature in her arms, the one that was biting and kicking as if it wanted to go back into the burning house. She didn't know what Timmy had become—some weird combination of child, adult, and animal, apparently. And she didn't know what kind of future he could possibly have.

But she did know, now, why she'd brought him out.

She looked at the childish face, the angry eyes full of hate. "Because my mom told me to take care of you," she whispered.

And then she was crying. She was holding him and sobbing. Timmy didn't try to hold her back, but he didn't bite her anymore either.

Still sobbing, Rashel looked over his head toward the house. Everything was burning. And Quinn was still inside. . . .

Then she saw a figure silhouetted against the flames. Two figures. One holding the other, half carrying it.

"Quinn!"

He was running toward her, supporting Nyala. They were both covered with soot. Nyala was swaying, laughing, her eyes huge and distant.

Rashel threw her arms around both of them. The relief that washed over her was almost more painful than the fear.

Her legs literally felt as if they had no bones—she was going to collapse at any second. She was tottering.

"You're alive," she whispered into Quinn's charred collar. "And you got her." She could feel Quinn's arm around her, holding hard. Nothing else seemed to matter.

But now Quinn was taking his arm away, pushing her along the road. "Come on! We've got to get to the wharf before they do."

In a flash, Rashel understood. She got a new grip on Timmy and turned to run toward the hiking path. Her knees were shaking, but she found she could make them move.

They lurched down the path in the wild grass, Quinn supporting Nyala, she carrying Timmy. Rashel didn't know how many vampires had made it out of the burning house—she hadn't seen any—but she knew that any who did would head for the dock.

Where she and Anne-lise had disabled the boats.

But as the wharf came into view, Rashel saw something that hadn't been there when she left it. There was a yacht in the harbor, swinging at anchor.

"It's Hunter's," Quinn said. "Hurry!"

They were flying down the hill, staggering onto the wharf. Rashel saw no sign of the werewolf she'd tied up earlier, but she saw something else new. An inflatable red dinghy was tied to the pier.

"Quick! You get in first."

Rashel put Timmy down and got in. Quinn lifted Timmy into her arms, then put Nyala in. Nyala was staring around her now, laughing in spurts, then stopping to breathe hard. Rashel put her free arm around her as Quinn climbed in the dinghy.

Every second, Rashel was expecting to see Hunter Redfern appear, blackened and smoldering, with his arms outstretched like some vengeful demon.

And then the tiny motor was purring and they were moving away from the wharf. They were leaving it behind. They were on the ocean, the cool dark ocean, freeing themselves from land and danger.

Rashel watched as the yacht got bigger and bigger. They were close to it now. They were there.

"Come on. We can climb up the swimming ladder. Come on, *fast*," Quinn said. He was reaching for her, his face unfamiliar in a mask of soot, his eyes intense. Absolutely focused, absolutely determined.

Thank God he knows what to do on a boat. I wouldn't. She let Quinn help her up the ladder, then helped Timmy and Nyala. Nyala had stopped laughing entirely now. She was simply gasping, looking bewildered.

"What happened? What—?" She stared toward the cliffs where orange flame was shooting into the sky. "I did that. Did I do that?"

Quinn had pulled up the anchor. He was heading for the cockpit. Timmy was crying.

Kneeling on the deck, Rashel held Nyala. Nyala's eyelashes were burned to crisp curls. There was white ash on the ends. Her mouth was trembling and her body shook as if she were having convulsions.

"I had to do it," she got out in a thick voice. "You know I had to, Rashel."

Timmy sobbed on. A motor roared to life. All at once they were moving swiftly and the island with its burning torch was falling behind.

"I had to," Nyala said in a choked voice. "I had to. I had to."

Rashel leaned to rest her head on Nyala's hair. Wind was whipping around her as they raced away. She held the tiny vampire in one arm and the trembling human girl in the other. And she watched the fire get smaller and smaller until it looked like a star on the ocean.

CHAPTER 17

Hunter's yacht was bigger than the powerboat Quinn had brought to the island. There was a salon down in the cabin and two separate staterooms. Right now, Timmy was in one of them. Nyala was in another. Quinn had put them both to sleep.

Quinn and Rashel were in the cockpit.

"Do you think any of the vampires got out?" Rashel said softly.

"I don't know. Probably." His voice was as quiet as hers.

He was filthy, covered with sand and soot, burned here and there, and wildly disheveled. He had never looked more beautiful to Rashel.

"You saved Nyala," she whispered. "And I know you did it for me."

He looked at her and some of the tense focus went out of his eyes. The hardness in his face softened.

Rashel took his hand.

She didn't know how to say the rest of what she meant. That she knew he had changed, that he was changing every minute. She could almost *feel* the new parts of his mind opening and growing—or rather, the old parts, the parts he'd deliberately left behind when he stopped being human.

"Thank you, John Quinn," she whispered.

He laughed. It wasn't a savage laugh, or a bitter laugh, or even the charming Mad Hatter laugh. It was just a real laugh. Tired and shaky, but happy.

"What else could I do?"

Then he reached for her and they were holding each other. They might look like two refugees from a disaster movie, but all Rashel felt was the singing joy of their closeness. It was such comfort to be able to hold on to Quinn, and such wonder to feel him holding her back.

A feeling of peace stole over her.

There were still problems ahead. She knew that. Her mind was already clicking through them, forming a dim checklist of things to worry about when she regained the ability to worry.

Hunter and the other vampires. They might still be alive. They might come looking for revenge. But even if they did . . . Rashel had spent her whole life fighting the Night World alone. Now she had Quinn beside her, and together they could take on anything.

Daphne and the girls. Rashel felt sure they were safe; she

trusted Anne-lise and Keiko. But once they got home, they'd be traumatized. They would need help. And someone would need to figure out what they should tell the rest of the world.

Not that anyone would believe it was real vampires who had kidnapped them if they said so, Rashel thought. The police would pass it off as a cult or something. Still, the girls know the truth. They may be fresh recruits for the fight. . . .

Against what? How could she be a vampire hunter now? How could she try to destroy the Night World?

Where could a reformed vampire and a burned-out vampire hunter go when they fell in love?

The answer, of course, was obvious. Rashel knew even as she formed the question, and she laughed silently into Quinn's shoulder.

Circle Daybreak. They'd become damned Daybreakers.

Granted, they weren't the type to dance in circles with flowers in their hair, singing about love and harmony and all that. But if Circle Daybreak was going to make any headway, it needed something besides love and harmony.

It needed a fighting arm. Somebody to deal with the vampires who were hopelessly evil and bent on destruction. Somebody to save people like Nyala's sister. Somebody to protect kids like Timmy.

Come to think of it, Circle Daybreak was where Nyala and Timmy belonged, too. Right now they need peace and healing, and people who would understand what they'd been through. I don't know, Rashel thought, maybe witches can help.

She hoped so. She thought Nyala would be all right—there was a kind of inner strength to the girl that kept her fighting. She wasn't so sure about Timmy. Trapped in a four-year-old body, his mind twisted by whatever lies Hunter had told him . . . what kind of normal life could he ever have?

But he was alive, and there was a chance. And maybe there were parts of his mind that were bright and warm and aching to grow.

Elliot and Vicky and the other vampire hunters. Rashel would have to talk to them, try to explain what she'd learned. She didn't know if they'd listen. But she would have to try.

"All anybody can do is try," she said softly.

Quinn stirred. He leaned back to look into her face. "You're right," he said, and she realized that he'd been thinking about the same things.

Our minds work alike, she thought. She had found her partner, her equal, the one to work and live and love with her. Her soulmate.

"I love you, John Quinn," she said.

And then they were kissing each other and she was finding in him a tenderness that even she hadn't suspected. But it made sense. After all, the opposite of absolute ruthlessness is absolute tenderness—and when you ripped the one away, you were left with the other.

I wonder what else I'll find out about him? she thought,

dizzy with discovery. Whatever it is, it's sure to be interesting.

"I love you, Rashel Jordan," he said against her lips.

Not Rashel the Cat. The Cat was dead, and all the old anger and the hate had burned away. It was Rashel Jordan who was starting a new future.

She kissed Quinn again and felt the beauty and the mystery of his thoughts. "Hold me tighter," she whispered. "I'm a little cold."

"You are? I feel so warm. It's spring tomorrow, you know."

And then they both were quiet, lost in each other. The boat sped on through the sparkling ocean and into the promise of the moonlit night.

The Night World
lives on in *Soulmate*,
by L. J. Smith.

The werewolves broke in while Hannah Snow was in the psychologist's office.

She was there for the obvious reason. "I think I'm going insane," she said quietly as soon as she sat down.

"And what makes you think that?" The psychologist's voice was neutral, soothing.

Hannah swallowed.

Okay, she thought. Lay it on the line. Skip the paranoid feeling of being followed and the ultra-paranoid feeling that someone was trying to kill her, ignore the dreams that woke her up screaming. Go straight to the *really* weird stuff.

"I write notes," she said flatly.

"Notes." The therapist nodded, tapping a pencil against his lips. Then as the silence stretched out: "Uh, and that bothers you?"

"Yes." She added in a jagged rush, "Everything used to

be so perfect. I mean, I had my whole life under control. I'm a senior at Sacajawea High. I have nice friends; I have good grades. I even have a scholarship from Utah State for next year. And now it's all falling apart . . . because of me. Because I'm going *crazy.*"

"Because you write notes?" the psychologist said, puzzled. "Um, poison pen letters, compulsive memo taking . . . ?"

"Notes like these." Hannah leaned forward in her chair and dropped a handful of crumpled scraps of paper on his desk. Then she looked away miserably as he read them.

He seemed like a nice guy—and surprisingly young for a shrink, she thought. His name was Paul Winfield—"Call me Paul," he'd said—and he had red hair and analytical blue eyes. He looked as if he might have both a sense of humor and a temper.

And he likes me, Hannah thought. She'd seen the flicker of appreciation in his eyes when he'd opened the front door and found her standing silhouetted against the flaming Montana sunset.

And then she'd seen that appreciation change to utter blankness, startled neutrality, when she stepped inside and her face was revealed.

It didn't matter. People usually gave Hannah two looks, one for the long, straight fair hair and the clear gray eyes . . . and one for the birthmark.

It slanted diagonally beneath her left cheekbone, pale strawberry color, as if someone had dipped a finger in blusher and then drawn it gently across Hannah's face. It was permanent—the doctors had removed it twice with lasers, and it had come back both times.

Hannah was used to the stares it got her.

Paul cleared his throat suddenly, startling her. She looked back at him.

"'Dead before seventeen,'" he read out loud, thumbing through the scraps of paper. "'Remember the Three Rivers—DO NOT throw this note away.' 'The cycle *can* be broken.' 'It's almost May—you know what happens then.'" He picked up the last scrap. "And this one just says, 'He's coming.'"